ALL THE DIRTY SECRETS

Kelsy T. Stubb

Contents

Junior Mitchie Halley is a cynical, unfriendly jerk. Despite having only one true friend at school, she is somehow categorized as one of the popular females. Behind her icy exterior is a rich history, but no one knows about it.

To put it bluntly, Chad is a bad boy. He has been kicked out of school multiple times for fighting, smokes anything he can find on campus, and sleeps with any lady who shows the slightest interest. They've known each other since they were little, but haven't had much of a conversation since elementary school.

In the meantime, Mitchie bumps into him in the hall, causing him to fumble his books and Mitchie to fumble hers. Mitchie takes his notes by mistake in her haste to get to her own.

Her discovery concerning Chad is documented in these notes. Something nobody would ever guess, and that he never wants anyone to find out.

Prologue

The first time I realized I had become a bitch was at the end of seventh grade.

Don't get me wrong, I had always been the good girl. I had always gotten great grades,was happy all the time, and had a perfect family life. That all changed in the middle of seventh grade.

My parents divorced, strike one. My mom took off with my siblings, strike two. And I started getting bullied, strike three. It wasn't the kind of bullying you see in movies where the pretty blonde talks crap because your breast aren't big enough, or you have glasses. Oh, how I wish it was that.

I was bullied by Chad Follet. How do I even begin to explain the jerk? He was tall for a seventh grader, he was already a good six feet by the end of middle school. He was pretty good looking, I guess. His brown hair was always cut short, but he had enough hair where he could style it. Honestly, the only part of him that wasn't very attractive were his cold, bottomless hazel eyes. The eyes that were lit with amusement when he would push me around in the hall ways.

The way Chad treated me wasn't the reason I became a bitch, it was only part of it. What turned me cold as ice was when he walked up to me the last week of school and said, and I quote;

"You motherless whore." I had lost it on him. Throwing myself at him as I tried to claw his eyes out. When the principal came, it was me who got expelled. My dad was confused of course, he was wondering why his perfect little girl had gotten expelled. That was the last time my dad ever saw his perfect little girl.

When I went back to school the next week, I wanted to show Chad just how much of a whore I was. I dressed as slutty as I could, caked myself in make up, and pretty much flirted with the whole football team. I was stupid for thinking it would be funny, that I would be able to shove it in his face. It only made things worse.

I stopped dressing in the clothes when I came back the next year, even though I looked the same, my attitude had completely changed.

The old me was gone. My friends had all turned their backs on me, my dad had thrown himself into his work, and I honestly could care less about my grades. The best part of the last year of middle school was that Chad Follet had disappeared.

That was four years ago. Chad came back at the start of freshman year, a completely different person. I couldn't have been more relieved when he didn't even give me the time of day. He was done messing with me, he had finally grown up. At least that's what I thought. . .

Chapter 1

My Paper Heart

"Louis Yeller is looking at you right now. Act normal." My best friend, Reagan Foster hissed, giving me a tight smirk. I rolled my eyes, shoving another spoon of pudding into my mouth.

"I'm serious, Mitch. He's like totally giving you the look. Go talk to him." She wiggled her eyebrows, nodding in encouragement. I reached over to pinch her chubby cheeks, snorting.

"I am not going to talk to him, Rae. Not unless you want to go talk to Karl." Her chubby cheeks grew red and she looked away from me. We must have looked pretty odd to everyone around us. The petite, pixie looking girl with black hair. And the overweight, blonde girl with an attitude. Everyone always gave us strange looks, to which we would just ignore or flip them off.

"Why do you hang out with her? To make yourself look better?" One of the "Mean" girls had asked a couple years ago. I had slapped her and walked away, not giving her the satisfaction of me replying. Honestly Reagan was the only person in this hellhole that understood me, that was just as messed up as I was. Despite her being a little overweight, she was gorgeous and I wished people would notice it.

"I told you I asked The Lover for advice a few weeks ago." Rae said, lifting her head back up. I snickered, twirling my fork in my hands.

"And what did she say?"

"To woman up and talk to him. But you guys don't seem to understand that it's harder then you think. Why would someone like him like someone like me?" She looked like she was about to start crying. I reached over and squeezed her hand. Karl was kind of an ass, not that I'd ever tell her that. He wasn't on a sports team or anything, he was just naturally popular. He loved everybody and everyone loved him.

"Maybe because you are gorgeous. Or because you have an amazing sense of humor. Any guy that can't see that is an idiot." She propped her face up on her hand and sighed.

"You have to say that, Mitchie. It's like in the best friend rulebook." We both giggled at that.

"You seriously should talk to him, Mitchie. You've had a crush on him since Freshman year." Rae said, turning the subject back to me.

"I am not. . ."

"I am finally back! Did you miss me?" I was cut off by the most self centered, egotistical person in the universe. Chad Follet. Everyone in the lunch room turned in his direction, all with googly eyes or grins.

"Chad, man!" Louis exclaimed, getting up. I watched him cross the room, his shaggy black hair a mess.

"Hey, Li. How was the game?" Did Chad have to be so obnoxiously loud? It's like he was trying to make my ears bleed.

"Look what the cat dragged in." Rae muttered, giving me a sympathetic look. I shrugged and turned back to the devil himself. I guess deep down, that the reason I didn't want to ask Louis out was because he was Chad's best friend. They literally did everything together, and I honestly didn't want to be anywhere near him.

"So I was told that someone here is throwing a party this weekend." Chad stated, looking around the room. I laughed quietly when he immediately looked over Rae and me.

"How was Physics?" I asked my best friend, turning away from everyone around us. Since the lunch room was almost silent, I knew everyone could hear me loud and clear. All heads snapped toward me, wondering why I was talking while their precious Chad Follet was.

"Is there something you'd like to say, McKayla?" Chad growled, his eyes on me. I stood up and tossed my food into the garbage. There was plenty of things I wanted to say, I just didn't want to get expelled.

"My name's Mitchie, asshole." I replied before stalking out of the room, flipping him off over my shoulder.

******

I was just about to doze off in Chemistry when the bell rang. I stood up, stretching. I started to walk toward the door when I felt someone grip my arm.

"Mitchie." The girl said, giving me a fake smile. She looked familiar, but I couldn't quite place where I knew her from.

"I was hoping you could make it to my party this weekend. Everyone that's anybody is going to be there."

"And. . .? You probably don't want Rae there so. . ."

"You can bring her! I mean, as long as she doesn't eat everything."

Everyone around the slutty blonde girl laughed. I shook my head, clenching my hand into a fist.

"I'll see if I can make it." I lied.

"Great! I hope to see you there!" I was just about to leave the room when I heard one of her friends whisper something.

"She's a bitch, Kim. Why the hell did you invite her?" I had to dig my nails into my palm to keep myself from turning around and showing her friend just how much of a bitch I really was. Instead I kept my composure and stormed out of the room.

"Mitch the bitch." That's what everyone had called me in eighth grade, thinking it was the funniest thing in the world.

"Mitchie, hey!" My head snapped up as I glanced around me. Louis was a few feet behind me, his hand on his knee.

"Hey." I mumbled. He gave me a toothy grin,, revealing his perfect teeth and leaned against the locker.

"I just wanted to apologize for what Chad said earlier. He was being an as. . ."

"It's fine, Louis. I've got to go." I tried to walk away but he caught me hand before I could.

"Okay, so maybe I lied about coming over here to apologize for Chad. I actually wanted to to talk to you." I hugged my text book against my chest, waiting for him to go on.

"Kim's throwing a party this weekend, as you know. I was hoping you could come with me." My jaw hit the floor. Had Louis Yeller just asked me out?

"So how about it?" He asked. I could feel a smile tugging on my lips as I nodded.

"Sure. Is. . . is Chad going to be there?"

"Probably, but don't worry. I won't let him near you." He winked, smiling again. I turned my face away so he couldn't see me blush.

"I'll see you on Saturday then." I finally said. He held out his phone, nodding at it.

"Give me your number. You know, so I can pick you up." I quickly put my number into his phone, then held it in my hand for a moment.

"You won't give it to the rest of the team, right? Or Chad?" I asked, skeptically.

"Of course not! I may be a jock, but I'm not an ass." He replied, clearly offended. I hesitantly handed him back his phone.

"I'm sorry, Louis. I. . . I don't trust a lot of people." I whispered. He gave me a sad look and started to back up.

"I get it, Mitchie. I'll see you on Saturday." He called over his shoulder as he jogged toward the locker rooms. I turned around and rushed toward the school entrance, searching for Rea through the window. Once I got outside I found her sitting on the curb, her face in her hands.

"Rea? What's wrong?" I sat down beside her, laying my hand on her back.

"Johnny is going to be late." I knew that wasn't what was bugging her.

"What's really going on, Rea?" She turned to me, her blue eyes shining in the sunlight.

"My parents are sending me to a boarding school. They think that I'm getting bullied too much here," She rolled her eyes, "I tried to tell them but they wouldn't listen. I'm leaving after Johnny picks me up." She sniffled, wiping tears from her cheeks. I looked away from her and down at the sidewalk.

"I'm so sorry I didn't tell you sooner, Mitchie. I. . . I thought they would change their minds. I'm so sorry." She cried. We sat there for a few minutes before a red Ferrari drove up. I didn't watch as Rea stood up and got in. I didn't even look up when she said goodbye. Just like that someone had left me. Again.

"Halley? What the hell are you doing out here?" Someone asked after a while. I could feel rain starting to fall on to my skin, I was glad that they would hide my tears.

"Halley I asked. . ."

"I'm not in the mood for your shit, Chad. Please just leave me alone." I snapped, my voice cracking. I waited to hear him laugh at me or snicker, but nothing came.

"My mom's at your house. I can drop you off if you want." I felt a cold, sarcastic laugh escape my lips.

"What's the catch? Are you just going to dump me off in an alley somewhere?" I replied.

"Whatever, Halley. Do you want a ride or not?" I slowly looked up, afraid to see the amusement in Chad's eyes. I found nothing but a cold stare. His hair was drenched, making it stick to his forehead.

"I. . . no. I don't want a ride from you. Just go." I finally repsonded. He stood beside me for a moment, before I felt him grab on to my arm.

"What the hell are you doing? Get your hands off of me!" I screamed, trying to push him away. I wished that there was still someone in the parking lot, but almost all the cars and people had vanished.

"You are stubborn." He muttered, dragging me. I tried to stop him, tried to find something to grab on to. Finally he whirled around and grabbed my shoulders, his eyes blazing with anger.

"Stop it! I am not going to dump you in some alley way, Mitchie. I am taking you to your damn house before you get sick." I stared in shock, letting my hands fall to my sides. That was the first time he had actually called me by my nickname, had actually talked to me like a civilized person.

"Why would you care if I got sick?" I whispered. He crossed his arms over his chest, tapping his foot impatiently.

"Are you done with your poor me crap? I do have places to be, you know."

"Then go! I don't need a ride from you." I crossed my own arms over my chest.

"Will you stop playing head games with yourself and get into my car, Halley? You know you don't want to walk home." I snorted and started to walk in the other direction.

"Watch me!" I yelled. I wrapped my arms around myself as I walked out of the parking lot. I could feel my teeth start chattering as I stared around me. The streets were dead, there was no cars except for an occasional one here and there. I thought about calling home, about calling my dad. But I knew better, I knew he'd snap at me and ask why I hadn't just asked one of my friends for a ride.

"Because I don't have any, not anymore." I whispered to myself, reaching up to wipe a tear from my cheek.

"Dammit, Mitchie. Get in my car." Chad growled. I turned to find his black Lexus beside me, the window rolled all the way down.

"Leave me alone!" I cried, stopping dead in my tracks. He slammed his head against his wheel and sighed.

"Please, Mitchie. Please get in my car." He said, exhausted. I stared down at my soaked clothes before sighing in defeat and climbing into the car. He shook his head to himself, not saying a word as we drove back to my house.

"We're here." He mumbled, leaning his head against the wheel. I got out of the car and stood outside of it for a moment.

"This doesn't change anything between us, Chad. I still hate you." For an instant I thought I saw guilt in his eyes, but it was gone as quick as it was there.

"The feelings mutual, Halley." He snapped before driving away.

Chapter 2

Change Your Mind

"It's going to be the party of the year."

"I know! Chad's going to be there. I can't wait to lose it to him!" I threw my hands over my mouth to keep myself from laughing. The girl beside the slutty blonde from yesterday, Kim, was talking so loud I could hear her from across the lunch room. The devil himself turned to her at the mention of his name and winked. I snorted and stabbed at my meatloaf with my fork.

"You look pissed." My head snapped up at the voice. Louis sat down beside me, his blue-green eyes filled with amusement.

"I'm fine." I muttered, looking away. I could tell he wasn't really aware of the fact that everyone in the lunch room had turned to look at us.

"I was wondering if you wanted to come and sit with me an. . ."

"I said I was fine, Louis. Please just leave me alone. I don't want to sit at your table." I stood up and moved away, setting my tray down when I was far enough away. I could hear whispers errupting around the room. Everyone obviously wasn't used to seeing their precious Quarterback get rejected.

"Just leave her alone, Li. She's being a bitch." Kim called out, smirking at Chad.

"Mitch the bitch." One of her bimbo friends said, the whole lunchroom started to laugh. Everyone, everyone except for Louis and. . . and Chad.

"Why don't you ditch the bitch?" Someone else yelled. I shook my head and shoved my food in the garbage, completely losing my appetite. I stalked out of the room, my eyes burning. I missed Rea, without her I felt like a weak little girl. As if God had heard my prayers my phone buzzed in my pocket.

Hey, Louis sent me a text. Said Kim was being a bitch again. Call me when you get home.

Louis knew Reagan? That was the first thought that went through my head. Reagan, the girl that hated jocks more then I did, was friends with the Quarterback?

"I am so confused." I whispered, shaking my head as I headed toward English.

******

I couldn't wait to get home after Chemistry. My head was pounding and I had started to get cramps in class.

"Oh my god! I'm so s. . . oh." I gasped as all of my books and notes flew from my hands and to the ground. Chad stood in front of me, his crystal blue eyes cold.

"Why don't you watch where you're going, Bitchie." He growled, pushing my arm away as I leaned down to pick up my notes. My eyes were burning again and I said the first thing that came to mind.

"You're such an ass, Chad." His eyes darkened and he pushed me. I fell back on to my butt and stared at him in shock. He had never, not even once, put his hands on me. Not even when we had got into it in seventh grade. He had always hurt me verbally, never physically.

"Don't you ever call me that again, Halley. Or I will make your life a living hell." He picked up the rest of his notes before kicking mine in my face and storming off. I looked down at the notes around me, tears streaming down my cheeks. I tried to keep myself from crying, but it resulted in more tears.

"Mitchie?" I quickly wiped the tears from my cheeks at the sound of Louis's voice. I couldn't let him see I was crying.

"Mitchie? Hey, what the hell just happened?" He knelt down beside me, already starting to gather my notes. I shook my head, avoiding eye contact as I pulled myself up.

"Nothing. I. . . I tripped and all of my stuff went flying everywhere." I lied, taking my notes from him. I thought I had escaped his questioning until he grabbed my chin in his hands and turned me toward him.

"Bullshit. I saw Chad over here. I don't know what he did, but I'm going to find out. I don't care whether it's from you or him." I sniffled and looked down.

"Nothing happened, Louis. Please just leave it alone."

"Just like I did for the last five years? Because "it's nothing", right? Chad pushing you around, calling you shit, it's just a big load of nothing?" He snapped, his eyes flickering toward the lockerooms.

"I. . . bye." I pushed him away and hurried to the school entrance, knowing that what I was about to go home too would be ten times worse.

****

"I said I'm okay, Rea. Now are you going to tell me how you know Louis?" I asked my best friend, pushing my black bangs out of my face.

"Well. . . um. . . he kind of asked me out before I left. He said Johnny had told him about me. He also said he thought I was cute." I immediately felt a sharp pain in my chest. Reagan was going to go out with Louis? She knew I liked him, she knew. . .

". . . . Mitchie? I know you used to have a crush on him but it's obvious that it's passed. I better go, my parents are still trying to talk to the boarding school about me coming back there. I hope they let me."

She hung up before I could say another word. I felt like I had been cut in half. Part of me was happy that Rea had finally had someone ask her out. Her self esteem had always been so low, I had always thought she'd end up in therapy or something. The other part of me wanted to walk over to her house and smack her. She knew I liked Louis, I liked him a lot. He had been my first crush, my first thing to hold on to since my mom and brothers left.

"McKayla! Get down here!" I winced at the sound of my fathers booming voice. I pushed my schoolwork aside and jogged out of my room. I stared around the living room in confusion, where had my Dad gone?

"Kay!" He yelled again. I clenched my shaking hand into a fist and walked into the kitchen. The first thing my eyes went to was his bloody hand and the millions shards of glass surrounding him.

"Dad? Dad, what happened?" I asked. I walked over and fell to my knees in front of him, reaching for his clenched hand. I opened his hand to find a shard of glass stuck in his palm.

"Daddy? What happened?" I repeated. He only groaned and slammed his head back against the counter.

"It's my fault, baby girl. I did it and. . ." He trailed off as I slowly pulled the glass from his palm. He reeked of liquor, which really wasn't that much of a surprise. He wouldn't touch any other alcohol, he said it was all crap.

"Dad, sit still. I have to clean your hand." I hissed, standing up to grab the gauze and Hydrogen Peroxide from the cabinet.

"I'm fine, McKayla. It's just a small cut." He tried to assure me, lifting his hand. He let out a cry as I grabbed a hold of it. I avoided eye contact with him as I cleaned his cut.

"You promised you'd stop drinking." I whispered. He was quiet for a moment. I looked up, afraid he might have passed out, only to find his dark eyes filled with guilt.

"I know, sweetie. I'm sorry. I never wanted you to be hurt or. . ." I blocked out the rest of his speech. It was what he said every single time he got hammered, every time he broke his promise.

"Come on, Dad. Let's get you to bed." I muttered, helping him up. I dragged him back to his room and helped him into bed. I stood in the middle of the room, my hands and blue t shirt covered in blood. Once I heard his breathing get heavier I walked out of the room and headed toward the bathroom. I cleaned myself up, pulling my shirt off on the way back to my room. I tossed on a clean t shirt and fell back on to my bed, tears in my eyes.

"How much more can you take, Mitchie? It's only a matter of time before he snaps and hurts you instead of himself." Reagan had told me more times then I could count. I had always told her he wouldn't hurt me, that he didn't even want to hurt himself.

He just wanted to escape the shitty reality he was living in. But she was right about how much more I could take. I had been living in the same reality with my dad since I was eight. The minute my mom walked out the door, she left not only her husband but her soon to be bipolar daughter. She didn't understand that when she left that Dad would go off the deep end, that he'd throw himself into alcohol and work.

"I hate you." I growled at the picture of my mom on the wall, throwing a pillow at the frame. It teetered for a minute before falling on to my dresser and shattering. I stared at the picture frame on my dresser before my eyes flickered to the pile of college brochures on my computer desk. I couldn't wait to get out of here, to get away from this crappy city. But leaving also meant that I had to leave my dad, he would have to live by himself. He wouldn't have anyone to help him to his room or clean him up when he got hammered, he would be alone. And as much as I hated doing all those things for my father, I knew I had too. I couldn't leave, and nothing in the world could change my mind.

Chapter 3

Swing, Swing

"Yeah, it totally sucks. But, I get to come visit in a couple weeks. I'm going on a date with Louis on Friday, but we can go out Saturday." My best friend said. I rolled my eyes, trying to think of an excuse.

"I can't. I have to go to Kim's party." I lied.

"Seriously, Mitchie? You can't stand her? Why the hell would you want to go to the party?" I was quiet for minute as I finished sorting my English notes.

"Dad started drinking again. It really doesn't matter, Rea. I have to go." I ended the call and tossed my phone on to my bed beside me. My eyes drifted toward a familiar pink notecard. It was the letter I had sent to The Lover a few weeks ago. The only reason I had done it was to please Rea. But why was it still with my notes, I know I sent it. My eyes drifted toward a folded piece of paper. I recognized the beautiful cursive writing. It was the letter Rea had sent. As I read it, I could feel my heart sink in my chest.

Lover,

I don't even know why the hell I'm writing to you, it's not like you'll actually respond. I. . . but I need to get something off my chest and this is the only way. My best friend likes this guy, like a lot. But the guy, he likes me. He asked me out and I kind of like him as well. What do I do? Do I tell my best friend that he asked me out? Do I go out without him? Thanks, R.F

That's what Rea had asked? She had asked The Lover if she should tell me about Louis?

"What the heck is going on?" I asked myself as I found a whole new pile of letters, all of them addressed to The Lover. I was about to throw them away when I saw folded note at the very bottom of the pile. I unfolded it and could feel tears pooling in my eyes.

I tried to believe that maybe you were hurting as much as I was. I tried to believe that you were bullying me because you couldn't find another outlet. But you took it to another level when you called me what you did yesterday, Chad. I hate you.

My hand was shaking so bad I dropped the note on to my bed. I had written the note to Chad at the end of the year and shoved it into his locker.

"I ran into Chad a couple days ago." I whispered to myself, pushing my memories out of my head. I couldn't have another fit of depression, not when my dad was drinking a lot again.

"That means he had these notes. . . why?" I asked myself aloud. Did the ass have to do everything in his power to ruin my life? Including stealing a private letter I had written to The Lover. And why the hell did he still have the note I wrote in middle school.

"Well, maybe I should find out." And I did. I climbed out of my bed, shoving all of the notes into a bag and jogging down the hall. I found my dad in the living room, watching UFC.

"Where are you going?" He asked. I held up the bag in my hand.

"I have to go over to the Follet's." I was glad that they lived down the street, that meant I didn't have to drive.

"Oh, will you tell Jill that I said I couldn't make it on Sunday." I nodded, not wanting to be nosy and ask why. I kissed him on the cheek before hurrying out of the house and into the cold weather. I walked pretty fast to the end of the street before crossing it. I hugged the bag to my chest as I knocked at the door. Ms. Follet opened the door and grinned.

"McKayla! What a surprise! How are you honey?" She gushed, pulling me into the warm house.

"I'm pretty good, I guess. I actually came over to talk to Chad. Is he here?" A frown immediately formed on her face. She had known what her son had done to me.

"Oh, is something going on with you two? Chad's been on his medications, I'm not sure why he would be acting up." Medications? Chad was on meds? Since when?

"No, ma'am. I just need to talk to him." I replied.

"All right, he's up stairs. You know the room." I nodded and jogged up the wooden stairs. As I edged closer to his room I could hear the heavy rock playing on his stereo.

"Chad!" I yelled, banging on the door. There was no response. I opened the door and peeked into the room. He had his face buried in his laptop.

"Chad!" I yelled again, this time he heard me. His head whipped toward me as he flew out of his computer chair. He reached for the remote to his stereo, his eyes bugging out of his head.

"How the hell did you get in here?" He asked, dropping the remote back onto his desk.

"Your mom loves me, Chad. Did you forget that she's my God Mother?" I snapped, raising an eyebrow. He gave me a cold glare and walked across the room to where I stood in his doorway.

"What do you want, McKayla?" He mumbled, impatiently.

"I found something that might belong to you." I handed him the notes in the plastic grocery bag, then crossed my arms over my chest. He opened the bag and began to read them.

"What the hell? How did you get these?" He growled, looking back up at me.

"I must have picked them up after you pushed me over." I said, equally pissed. He took both of my wrists in his hands.

"You aren't going to tell anyone about this, right? Because you know what I'm capable of, Mac." The nickname caused both of us to stiffen. He hadn't called me Mac since elementary school, when we would spend everyday at each others houses.

"I. . . I didn't mean to say that." He sputtered, shaking his head. I looked down at his hand, which were still holding mine, before sighing.

"Tell anyone what, Chad? I don't really want to deal with this right now. I'm not in the mood for your mood swings." I looked up at him, exhausted.

"You mean you are so naive that you don't understand? McKayla, I'm The Lover." I stared at him for a second, seeing if he was serious, before I started busting up.

"You The Lover? Yeah right! Nice one Nic!" My eyes grew wide at the name. I winced, waiting for him to push me or shove me.

"Why are you cringing? I'm not going to hurt you, Mitchie. Don't you think I've hurt you enough over the last few years?" Wow, had I just heard remorse in his voice?

"You're serious, then? Y. . . you're The Lover? You mean all these years you've let people think you were a girl?" He smirked.

"Not exactly. My sister was it before I came, so it was a girl. But her last wish before she went across country was that I did it for her. So I did, I became The Lover." I smiled, nodding. We were actually having a normal, civilized conversation.

"I better leave. I. . . don't worry, I won't tell anyone. Who would I tell anyway?" I muttered, bitterly. I backed out of the room and shut the door behind me. When I reached the final step I found Ms. Follet sitting on the couch.

"Is everything all right?" She asked once she saw me. I nodded.

"Everything is fine. I just had to return something to Chad." I replied. We said our goodbyes before I walked toward the door and left. I stopped on the last step and turned around to look at the house. I knew that the conversation I had just had with Chad had been a one time thing. Tomorrow we would go back to school and he would be a total ass and I'd go back to being a bitch. That's just how it was. And as much as I hated to admit it, I really didn't want that to change.

Chapter 4

Gives You Hell

"We're going out later, to a dance at my sister's school. Do you want to come?" Kim asked me, smiling. I smiled back, nodding.

"Sure." Somehow I had let Louis talk me into sitting with them. Even with Chad glaring at me the whole time from the other side of the table, I had managed to stick around the whole lunch period.

"Awesome! Do you need a dress or. . ."

"I can borrow one from my mom." I lied. My mom had left a lot of her clothes behind, not caring what my dad did with them. My dad, being who he is, kept all of her clothes their closet. There had to be a dress in there somewhere.

"You do understand that there will be tons of horny middle school boys there, right?" Louis asked, smirking. Kim slapped his arm and a giggle escaped my lips.

"We can show them what they can look forward too coming to high school." One of Kim's friends said, winking at me. I snickered and stabbed my fork into the still half frozen meatloaf.

"Well, I for one, want to see how this plays out. I'm going too. What about you Chad?" I looked up at him from the corner of my eye. Please don't come. Please don't. . .

"Sure. I'm not going to miss out on Bitchie being humiliated."

"Fuck you, Chad." I replied, shoving my food into the trash. I had lost my appetite.

"I know you want too." He called after me. I flipped him off over my shoulder without turning to look at him. I was afraid that if I did I would claw his eyes out. I heard him call something else after me but it was cut off by the cafeteria doors shutting loudly behind me.

*****

"Miss Halley and Mr. Follet!" I swear the gym teacher had it out for me. He had since freshman year. He knew I hated Chad, yet he always paired me with him.

"Go ahead and start." I glared at Chad as I sat down on the mat.

"Long time no see, Bitchie."

"I'll kick you in the face if you call me that one more time." I growled. He held his hands up in surrender, a smug smile on his face. I rolled my eyes and fell back on to the mat.

"Hey, this isn't such a bad view." He said, trying to look up my gym shorts. I pulled my leg from his grip and kicked him in the chest.

"Ouch." He mumbled, rubbing his chest. The gym teacher gave us a look and Chad went back to holding my feet.

"Say another word and I'll kick you in the face." I hissed, before starting to do sit-ups.

"You wouldn't dare to mess up my beautiful face." I snorted and did another sit up.

"You'd be surprised of what I'm capable of, Chad. Don't forget that I know your little secret." I whispered then winked. He didn't say anything else for the rest of gym glass except a few sex innuendos.

"If you even speak a word of it I will kill you. . ." I held my hand up, stopping Chad from continuing.

"Then here is a few things you need to do. I won't say a word if you follow these rules. Stop calling me Bitchie. Stop being a dick to me in front of your friends. And if I hear one more sex innuendo come out of your mouth I'll make you wish you had never said a word to me." He stared at me in shock as I flipped my hair over my shoulder dramatically and stalked out of the gym.

***

"Are you trying to blackmail me?" Chad snarled, slamming my locker shut so I had to face him.

"Maybe." I replied.

"You better think again, Halley. Because I know your dirty little secret." I gave him an innocent look.

"What do you mean?" I asked. He stepped closer to me and slammed his hand against the lockers, trapping me.

"Just remember that some secrets are better left untold." He said, before turning around and walking off.

I stared after him, my mouth still hanging open. He couldn't possibly know about my dad, could he? No, no. He was probably talking about something stupid, like my crush on Louis or something. That had to be it, it had to be.

****

I sat on my bed, running my hands along the midnight blue dress I was wearing. I was starting to regret agreeing to go to the dance. Even the little girls there would get more attention, more guys then I would.

"McKayla! Your friend is here!" My dad shouted. I stood up, grabbing my purse from my computer chair. I stopped in front of the mirror on the way out. I didn't look that bad, but I didn't look nearly as good as my mom had in the same dress either. It hugged me, making my curves more predominant. I had curled my hair so it fell in black ringlets around my face, which had very little make up on it.

"Kay!" My dad yelled. I shut my light off and jogged down the hall. I stood in shock when I saw Louis and Chad at the door. Kim had told me she was going to pick me up.

"Wow." Louis whispered, taking in my appearance. I blushed and bowed my head as I headed toward the door.

"Can I please talk to my daughter alone?" My dad asked the boys. They both nodded and stepped outside of the house.

"Why the hell are you wearing that dress?" I shrugged, trying to ignore the liquor bottle in his hand.

"It's not like it was being used. I needed it. . ."

"For what? So you can go walk around and be a whore? You know that was the only time your mother wore that dress, Kay. When she was feeling like she wanted some. . ."

"Stop it! I am not her, Dad! I'm. . ."

"There is two boys out there that will probably end up fuck. . ." I did the stupidest thing I had ever done, I slapped him. His eyes darkened and he slapped me. The minute I let out a sound, his whole expression changed.

"McKayla. . ." I shook my head, rushing toward the door.

"Kay, please come. . ." I was relieved when I found Chad leaning against the door frame. His eyes immediately went to where my hand was covering my aching cheek.

"Mitchie. . ." He whispered, I jogged down the steps before he could continue. I wanted to get as far away from the house as possible.

"McKayla! Get your ass back here and. . ." He trailed off when Chad turned to him. I felt Louis grab my arm as Chad grabbed my dad by the collar of his shirt, growling something into his ear.

"Hey, let's go. Kim's waiting for us." Louis whispered, pushing my hand away from my throbbing cheek. I watched Chad shove my dad back and jog toward us. He didn't say a word as we got into the car, but I knew. I knew that he really did know my secret. He knew about my dad, he knew about the holes in the walls inside my house and the reason they were there. And even if it was for an instant and it was the wrong person I should be feeling it for, I felt cared for. I didn't feel alone.

"Does he do it a lot?" Chad asked, no emotion in his voice. I looked up from the back seat, shrugging.

"Enough. He. . . he's never hit me before." I replied. Chad turned to face me, his blue eyes cold.

"The next time he lays a hand on you, tell someone." I bit my lip, nodding. I was glad that Louis was driving so slow, because honestly, I didn't really want to go back home.

Chapter 5

Too Far Gone

I sighed as I watched Rae and Louis dancing. Apparently Louis had invited Rae, thinking she wouldn't come, but she had. She'd walked right passed me like I wasn't even there, and honestly that was what hurt me the most. We had been best friends since middle school, when we were both so screwed up that we didn't think anything could make us feel any worse. She was my best friend, in some weird way my sister and soulmate. Not in the weird love kind of way, but in a way that made me feel like she was my other half, the better half of myself.

"Penny for your thoughts?" I grimaced at the sound of Chad's voice.

"In your dreams." I muttered. He didn't take the hint but sat down in the chair beside me.

"It must hurt, seeing your best friend dancing with your crush." He stated. I turned to him just so he could see me roll my eyes.

"Stop acting like it doesn't effect you, Mitchie. I know it does. I read your letter and. . ."

"It wasn't the truth. I only wrote it to please Regan. Just drop it." I snapped, taking a sip from my sprite.

"Mitchie. . ." I recognized the tone in his voice. It was the same tone my dad used when he was sober and was about to apologize.

"Don't, Chad. I don't want to hear how fucking sorry you are for treating me like crap the last five years." I looked away from him, not wanting him to see how miserable I looked.

"I know, Mitchie. No amount of apologizes will ever make it up to you. I was going to ask you if you wanted to dance." He gestured toward the dance floor, where tons of kids were dancing awkwardly. I could feel my jaw drop as I turned back to him. Was Chad Follet asking me to dance?

"I. . . there are much prettier girls for you to dance with here, Chad." I finally responded, shaking my head.

"Maybe. But I want to dance with you. Now lets go." He held his hand out to me and I took it with a long sigh. He fixed his black tie and led me toward Louis and Rae.

"Just so you know, Louis can't dance. You aren't missing much." I giggled as we stopped beside them. Rea and Louis stared at us in shock but didn't say anything.

"I'm not joking. I have never seen someone dance so bad in my life." He joked. I shook my head at him as he spun me around.

"You are such a jerk, Chad." Even if it was the truth, I couldn't help but wrap my arms around his waist and lay my head against his chest. Because I knew what he was trying to do, I knew he was trying to take my mind off my dad and Louis.

"Thank you, Chad." I whispered. He smiled.

"No problem. It's the least I can do." I had never heard someone sound so regretful in my life.

*****

"Are you sure you're going to be okay?" Louis asked again from the front seat as we pulled up to my house. I glanced at the dark house, sighing.

"He should be asleep. I'll be fine." Louis gave Chad a weird look then nodded in the back seat at me.

"Rae wanted me to tell you she was sorry and that she. . ."

"If she wants to say it, let her say it to my face." I growled coldly. He turned away as he parked the car in front of my house. I climbed out and was surprised when Chad followed me out.

"What are you doing?" I asked, staring at him skeptically. He gave me a slight shrug and pointed at my house.

"I'm going to walk you to the door and make sure the ass doesn't hit you again." I didn't say a word as he walked me up the driveway.

"Kim said you were coming to her party next Saturday."

"Yeah, so?" I replied, crossing my arms over my chest.

"I don't think you should go." I stopped and whirled around to face him. His blue eyes were dark and on me, but his face had been pulled into an emotionless mask.

"Excuse me? Why not? I finally get invited to a party and Mr. Bad Boy doesn't want me to go? I'm done letting you walk all over me, Chad. Just. . ."

"I don't think you should go, McKayla. Okay? It's not that I don't think you deserve to go, I just think it's a bad idea to go to her party." He muttered.

"Why?" I questioned, getting ready to leave him right then and there in the middle of my driveway.

"Just remember that I told you not to go." And with that he walked back down to Louis's car and they drove off without another word.

**

"Mitchie." I groaned and buried my face deep into my pillow. I sat up, my eyes shooting open when I realized that the voice didn't belong to my dad. I looked up at the two people in my room, pulling my blanket over me. Rae stood in front of my bed, her eyes glistening. Louis stood in the doorway, staring back and forth between the two of us.

"So I just recently learned that you have a crush on me Mitchie." Louis stated, walking over to my bed. I shook my head, my cheeks and eyes burning from embarrassment.

"I did. I don't anymore." How could Rae tell Louis about my crush on him? Didn't she know how to keep a secret?

"I think you're lying. Mitchie, I can't even begin to imagine how much Rae and I together must hurt you. I didn't ever want to be the reason you guys stopped being friends." He added. My eyes flickered to Rae who had started to cry.

"I'm so sorry, Mitchie. I didn't know your dad. . . and I should have told you about Louis. I'm so so sorry." She sat on the edge of my bed, wiping the tears from her cheeks.

"I. . . it's fine, Rae." I said quietly, reaching over to put hand on her shoulder. She smiled through her tears, but it was Louis who spoke.

"I know Chad was trying to convince you not to go to Kim's party last night, "He paused, sitting in my computer chair, "and I agree. I don't think it's a great idea for you to go." I could feel my hands clench into fists.

"Can you tell me why? I think both of you should stay the hell out of my business. Why do you care if I go to the party or not?" Louis, being the extremely nice guy he was, didn't get mad. Instead he pulled himself up and walked toward the door. He stopped just outside of it and I could see just how tense he was.

"I don't care, Mitchie. It was Chad that wanted me to try and convince you not to go. You should talk to him about it." Then he was gone. I turned back to my best friend, who looked just as confused as I felt.

"Chad is all up in your business? Speaking of the devil, what the hell was going on with you two last night? You were like. . . flirting." She said, staring at me patiently. I smiled, trying to keep myself from busting up.

"We weren't flirting, Rea. And I don't know why he is suddenly so interested in my life." I responded. She frowned.

"Do you think it's because he knows about your da. . ."

"Maybe. But this is Chad Follet we are talking about, Rea. He's hated my guts since middle school. He must have some secret motive." She nodded in agreement, still looking a little confused. Finally her green eyes flickered to me and she asked a good question.

"And what are you going to do about it?" She asked.

"I'm going to try and find out what it is."

Chapter 6

Stab My Back

One. Two. Three.

"McKayla! Where are you going?" My dad growled, pushing the glass of water in front of him off the table. I watched it fall to the ground, my eyes burning.

"I'm going to a party." I whispered. The last week and a half had gone by in a lonely blur. Chad wouldn't talk to me, Louis attempted too, and everyone at the table would always try to include me, pitiful looks in their eyes.

"A party? Who's party?" My dad asked, stopping in front of me. I took a step back, pulling my keys out of my purse.

"A friends. I'll be back later." I hurried out of the house before he could stop me. Once I was in my car I laid my head against the wheel, hoping that the rest of the night would be better.

****

"You can do this, Mitchie." I said to myself, staring at Kim's house. There were teens walking around inside and out, some were even sitting on the porch making out. My gaze stopped when it landed on a familiar royal blue Ferrari. Chad's royal blue Ferrari.

"Just remember that I told you not to go." I could hear Chad telling me. Why did he not want me here so bad? I had tried to get him to talk to me a couple times this week but he had either blew me off or walked away.

"Come on." I muttered to myself and got out of the car. I walked up the driveway as slowly as possible. A few drunk guys whistled and yelled after me as I walked passed them. Which only earned them the finger from me.

"Oh don't be a bitch, Mitche!" One of the guys yelled. I rolled my eyes and jogged up the stairs into the house. My eyes immediately met familiar cold blue ones.

"I didn't think you were going to show up after everyone warning you off." Chad snapped. I grinned up at him.

"Hello to you too." I replied sarcastically. He scoffed and set the red cup in his hands on the table.

"I really think you should leave, Mitchie." I tried to walk away but he gripped my arm tightly.

"Mitchie. . ." I shoved his arm away and walked toward the kitchen.

"Oh my god! You're here! Come on, I want to show you something." Kim screeched. I didn't even have a chance to speak before she dragged me down the hall and toward the backyard. A bunch of people were scattered around the pool, but they all looked up when they saw me. I felt something tug at the back of my shirt and I suddenly regretted wearing a thin shirt.

"Listen, Bitchie. You didn't really think I would invite you to my party, did you?" Kim said, ripping my shirt from my body. My hands immediately reached up to cover my chest. I turned to find some jock standing beside her smirking.

"You think you are going to replace me, don't you? But listen here, sweetie. No one will ever replace me. You keep trying to take Chad and Louis away but they would never like some little ugly bitch like you. Even your fat friend is prettier than you are." I could feel heat rush to my cheeks as my eyes began to burn. I should have listened to Chad. I should have listened. . .

"What? Can you not speak now? Is it because everyone is looking at your ugly ass half naked?" She shoved me back and I stumbled backwards and fell into the pool. I resurfaced to find everyone laughing and a few girls patting Kim on the back. I let out a growl and pulled myself out of the water. I stomped over to where Kim stood and smacked her across the face.

"I may be ugly, but at least I'm not some fake little slutty whore that everyone's had sex with. I least I don't have a fucking STD because I slept with some fifty year old man at a dinner party my dad threw." I yelled. Everyone went quiet. Kim's eyes grew dark and shocked.

"H. . . how would you know that?" She stuttered. The boy behind her stared at her in horror.

"You have an STD?" He gasped. I shoved Kim back.

"You are a fucking whore." I hissed. She caught the back of my bra and let out another screech.

"What are you going to go back home where Daddy will beat you?" I could feel my whole body grow tense. I flipped around and shoved her as hard as I could. She fell on her butt, staring up at me.

"At least I didn't have sex with him for fun." I stalked away from her, flipping everyone that called after me off. All eyes were on me as I walked through the house, not even caring to cover my chest anymore.

"Bitchie! Bitchie! Bitchie!" I stopped in the living room once everyone started chanting. I couldn't hold back the tears in my eyes anymore and I ran out of the house. I was immediately aware that someone was chasing after me.

"Mitchie! Stop!" I ignored the voice.

"Mac, please!" The nickname caused me to trip over a rock and fall in the street. My hands went to my bloody knee as my vision began to blur.

"Mac, don't. . ." I looked up at Chad, giving him the worst glare I could possibly give him.

"Don't you ever call me that! Ever!" I cried. He knelt down in front of me, but I slid back, covering myself with the dirt from the road.

"Dammit, Mitchie. Come here." He held his arms open, waiting for me to jump into them. I shook my head, starting to hyperventilate.

"I hate you! I. . . you knew about it! You knew!" I buried my face in my hands, rocking back and forth.

"Chad, man! What the fuck are you doing with the crazy bitch? Look at. . ." Chad stood up and swung at the boy behind him repeatedly. Finally a couple seniors pulled the two guys apart.

"Fuck man! You're as crazy as she is!" The guy snapped before turning around and walking back toward the house.

"Mitchie, let me drive you home and. . ."

"I don't want to go home." I whispered. I wiped the tears from my eyes and cheeks, sniffling.

"Okay, I'll take you back to my place. You can sleep on the couch, my mom won't mind." I shook my head, still rocking back and forth.

"No. I don't want to be some charity case. Stop looking at me like that!" I knew that my bipolar attitude was scaring Chad because he stared at me in horror.

"Mac, stop. It's okay." He fell to his knees in front of me, not caring if they were going to be completely covered in crap.

"Mac, I promise everything will be fine." He pulled his black t shirt over his head and held it out to me. My eyes were to focused on his abs for me to see his hand.

"Put this on or you're going to freeze to death." I took the shirt from him hesitantly, peeling my eyes from his bare chest.

"Thanks." I mumbled as I pulled the shirt over my head. It hung off my body loosely.

"Let's go get something to eat." I was surprised when he walked me over to my car instead of his own. When he saw the look I was giving him he gave me a half smile.

"I can pick it up tomorrow or something." He took the keys from my hand and held the door open for me. I stood frozen for a minute, looking at the ground.

"Why are you being so nice to me?" I asked.

"Because everyone else is being an asshole. Plus I know what it's like being talked down to and shit." I looked up in surprise. He wouldn't meet my eyes.

"I haven't always been popular, Mitchie. You know that. Now lets go before I do something stupid." I slid into the car without a word. He slammed the door shut before yelling something across the yard.

I watched as some guy flipped Chad off and he returned the action. He walked around the car and got in.

"Next time I see that stupid ass you better be there so I don't attack him." He said. I nodded slowly as he started the car. I leaned my head against the cold window, dreading the thought of going to school on Monday. And dreading going home even more.

"Are you okay?" Chad asked as we walked up the stairs to his house. I gave him the most sarcastic smile I could.

"Just perfect." I replied. He rolled his eyes and unlocked his door. His mom immediately rushed to the door when she saw me.

"Oh, darling! Mrs. Yeller just called me! I'm so sorry sweetheart!" She pulled me into an unfamiliar motherly embrace. I buried my face in her sweater, finally falling apart.

"How dare you Chad! I can't believe you would let her go!" She screamed at her son once I pulled away. He winced at her yelling before running a hand through his brown hair.

"I know, Mom. I'm sorry. I should of. . ."

"You bet! This poor girl is. . ." I pushed passed Chad and jogged out of the house. I threw my hands over my ears as I walked quickly toward my house as memories started to flicker in my mind.

"You piece of shit! How dare you lay a hand on my son!" My mom screeched, pushing David behind her. I crawled out from where I was hiding in the pantry. I darted toward my parents, but David caught me in his arms as I screamed at them.

"Stop! No more fighting! Mommy! Daddy! Stop!" I cried, scratching at my older brother's arms.

"I hate you! You don't even know how much, Jack. I am sick and tired of you constantly getting drunk and doing whatever you feel. I'm taking the kids and leaving." She turned to face the three of us, David, Danny, and me.

"Go pack your stuff, boys." She ripped me from David's grip, making him glare at her.

"Mom, don't you dare think about leaving. . ."

"I can't deal with her. She's annoying and useless just like her father." The words that left my mother's mouth caused me to kick her away from me and I fell to the ground with a thud.

"You bitch! How dare you throw my daughter like that!" My dad picked me up, holding me against him. I tried to ignore the smell of the liquor on his clothes as I buried my face against him.

"Mom! We have to take her, we. . ." Danny argued, grabbing at my mom's dress. She pushed him away and shook her head at my brothers.

"Get in the car! Go!" She growled at them. My dad tightened his grip on me and walked my mom to the door.

"Don't you ever think about coming back. Get out!" He slammed the door even before she was outside of the door.

"McKayla, it's okay. She's gone." My dad whispered, setting me down. I grabbed on to his legs and started sobbing.

"Mitchie!" Chad's voice snapped me out of my thoughts. I looked to down to find myself standing in the middle of the street. Chad was a few feet away, his hands on his knees as he gasped for breath.

"Stay away." I whispered, stepping back and tripping over my own foot.

"Kay? Is that you?" I could hear my dad ask from behind me groggily. I backed away from Chad, nodding as I ran over to my dad. I threw myself into his arms and started to cry. He held me there, asking me what was wrong.

"Let's get you inside." He said, and we walked back into my dark house.

******

"Good morning, Sleeping Beauty." I made a growling noise at the voice.

"Go away, Chad!" I heard him chuckle behind me.

"But I need your help. I need you to help me respond to these letters." I pried my eyes open to find Chad sitting on my bed and waving a binder.

"Go home." I muttered, throwing myself back against my pillow. He sighed and poked my stomach until I looked up in annoyance.

"What do you want, Chad?" I asked, irritated.

"I told you. I want you to help me with these letters." He waved the binder in my face again. I mumbled something under my breath before taking the binder from me.

"Why do you need my help? Are you The Lover?" He shrugged, taking a chocolate bar from my stash in the nightstand.

"I need answers that sound girly if I don't want people to find out." He answered, grinning. I hit him over the head with the binder, he snorted and pushed me backwards playfully.

"Please, Mitchie. It'll be fun. We can even go get coffee or something afterward." I stared at him in surprise.

"Aren't you afraid of people seeing you with Bitchie?" I asked bitterly. He laid back on my bed, crushing my legs.

"Ouch! Chad! Okay, okay! I'll do it!" He grinned and sat back up, only to be kicked off the edge of my bed.

"You'll get a kick out of this first one. It's Kim. And I'm going to let you say whatever the hell you want." I could feel a smile tugging at my lips.

"Are you sure?" I asked. He plopped back down on the bed beside me, shoving the whole chocolate bar into his mouth.

"Positive."

Chapter 7

One More Sad Song

"She actually came to school? Wow."

"Why the hell is Chad with her?"

"Oh look the bitch came back!" That's all I heard throughout the day on Monday. Chad, being the annoying guy he is, stuck by me all day and even dragged me out to Louis's football practice after school.

"Mitchie! Hey!" Louis said, breathless. I waved at him shyly and he stopped in front of us.

"I'm so sorry that Kim. . ."

"Just drop it, Louis. It's fine." I muttered, shaking my head.

"Okay. So I heard you beat the crap out of Peter." Louis said, turning his attention to Chad who was currently trying to open a package of Doritos.

"Yeah. He was being an ass." I sighed, grabbing the bag and pulling it open.

"Sounds like someone else we know." Louis stated. Chad flipped him off before tossing a chip into his mouth.

"I may be an ass, but I'm not a cold hearted piece of shit like he is." Louis stared at his best friend in shock. Chad seemed unaffected and held the Doritos out to me, probably asking if I wanted one.

"I thought you and Peter were friends. . . does this have something to do with what Kim wrote you in the letter. . ." I gasped, dropping the chip in my hand to the ground.

"You know?" I asked Louis.

"Know what?" He looked bored.

"About Chad being The Lover." I whispered, moving closer to him so I was sure no one could hear.

"Of course I know, Mitchie. He's my best friend. And now that I know you know, I take it you were the one that wrote the letter back to Kim." He guessed. I smiled sheepishly and took a step back.

"I mean, the little bitch had it coming, Li." Chad cut in. Louis sighed in defeat and glanced back over his shoulder.

"I guess so. I better get back to practice before Coach Henson kills me." He waved goodbye to us before jogging off.

"So do you think Ol' Daddy is going to drink tonight?" Chad asked as we headed out toward the parking lot.

"Probably. He's been drinking every night for the last few weeks." I said quietly, not wanting anyone to hear our conversation.

"You could stay at my place if you want. I promise I won't fight with my mom again." He said, a grin slipping across his face. I nodded and stopped directly in front of my car.

"I'll see you later, then. Rae was supposed to call me like an hour ago so I'll probably call her back before heading over to your place." He gave me a dashing smile before walking away. Once I was situated in my car I laid my head against the wheel. Why was I trusting Chad so much? Was it because he made me feel normal? Because he actually knew the real me and not the person that everyone makes me out to be? Could. . . could I be starting to like him?

"Nah, he's just an idiot friend." I muttered to myself, pulling out of the school parking lot.

****

I was blasting my radio when my heart started racing. The song that came on the radio made my eyes burn.

"Light's will guide you home. And ignite your bones. I, will try, to fix you."

It had been my favorite song as a child, my mom had played it all the time. She had been one of Coldplay's biggest fans, and this had been her favorite song of all time. I could remember going over to Chad's and shoving the CD with the song on it into his hands, telling him that he would fall in love with the song.

"What the hell?" I whispered, turning my radio down when I saw the white mini-van parked in my driveway. I pulled my car over by the curb and hurried up to my house. I threw the door open to find my dad sitting on the loveseat, his face buried in his hands. My eyes slowly drifted to who sat across from him on the leather couch. It was David and his wife Destiny.

"Mitchie!" He grinned, getting up. I let him pull me into his warm embrace, but I don't think I had ever felt so cold.

"Dave." I whispered. I was about to continue when something tugged at my pants and a noise came from down the hall.

"Ellie, let go!" Destiny growled, pulling her daughter off of me. I stared down the hall only to be greeted by familiar dark blue eyes.

"Danny." I said, taking in his appearance. He and David had always looked similar, they had looked like our dad. Both of them had dark black hair and bright blue eyes, my mom had said it was because my grandparents on both sides had been Welsh.

"You're so handsome." My mom had always told Danny. He really was. He had always looked older than David, even though they were almost three years apart. It could be because he stood a good three or four inches taller, or because he was always having to shave his beard, even when he had only been thirteen.

"Mitchie!" He yelled, running over to me and picking me up. I stood frozen, just as I had with David. Danny set me down, staring at me in confusion.

"Aren't you happy to see us?" He asked, hurt. I tried to smile, but failed.

"You left me." I whispered. His eyes darkened and he shook his head, causing his black hair to fall into his eyes.

"No, Mom left you. We tried, Mitchie. We tried to. . ."

"Bullshit! You left with her, you didn't stay with me! You could have forced her to take me!" I yelled, sniffling. He made a growling sound in the back of his throat.

"You're so lucky you didn't have to live with the psychotic bitch. All she did was force us to do shit, and everything she said was horrible about dad, she turned into! She almost died two years ago, Mitchie. From mixing drugs and alcohol. Dave and I had to put her into a Insane Asylum, she hates us for it. So feel lucky you didn't come with us that night." I stared in horror, grabbing on to my couch so I didn't fall.

"N. . .no." I whispered. He nodded.

"I. . . is she bi-polar?" I said, my heart starting to race.

"Maybe. Why? Mitchie, you aren't. . ."

"She is." My dad answered, cutting me off.

"I bet it's your fault too asshole." Danny hissed. Destiny gave him a dirty look, pointing at her and Dave's daughter.

"Does he hit you?" David asked, grabbing on to my shoulder. I looked between my two brothers, shutting my eyes.

"N. . . no. He. . . he did the other night. He. . . but it was because I hit him. He didn't mean. . ."

"You laid a hand on her!" Danny looked about ready to launch himself at our dad but was stopped by David.

"Dan, stop. Mitchie, we came here for a reason. We wanted to know if you wanted to move back to Colorado with us. Danny's starting college, but he's bought a house and everything that you could sleep in. And you're always welcome to stay with Destiny and me." I couldn't believe the words that were leaving his mouth. They were offering me a way out of this hell hole? I could finally leave. . .

"Kayla?" My dad said, snapping me out of my thoughts. He sat on the loveseat, his eyes bloodshot. I let out a sigh.

"I can't leave, Dave. I can't leave Dad and. . ."

"Don't feed me that. We can have someone come stay with Dad or maybe we could put him into a community home. You think I don't talk to Mrs. Follet, but I do. She told me what happened the other day, Mitchie. I don't want you staying here." David replied, squeezing my elbow. I bit down on my quivering lip and wrapped my arms around him.

"C. . . can I think about it?" I stuttered. He pulled away and grinned.

"Of course. We'll be in town for a week or two. Elle has never been to Disneyland." I nodded and looked toward my seven year old niece, she waved.

"I'll call you tomorrow to check on you." David whispered, obviously referring to our dad. I smiled and he kissed my forehead. Danny hugged me quickly too before Destiny pulled me into a hug.

"I'd love to have you around, Mitchie. Dave's told me so much about you." I grinned at her, then watched them all leave. I shut the door behind them and laid my head against the door, ignoring the questioning look my dad was giving me. Did I want to go?

"I do." I whispered aloud before jogging down the hall and to my room.

Chapter 8

Kids In The Street

"Chad. We were talking about Chad, not Louis." Rae said, her eyes growing wide in suspicion.

"Whatever. What's the difference?" I said a little to quickly. She stared at me, her mouth opening.

"Oh, crap! You like Chad!" I pushed my food away from me, gawking at her.

"What? No I don't! We. . . we're just friends." I replied. She rolled her eyes.

"You like him, Mitchie. Because he's the only one in this shitty town that will even give you the time of day." I avoided her eyes and got up.

"Whatever, Rea. Maybe I wouldn't have to rely so much on Chad if you were still my best friend." I slammed my money on the table and stormed out of the diner, not even caring to look back to see her reaction.

***

"Are you seriously singing Boulevard of Broken Dreams?" I continued to walk down my street, ignoring Chad.

"Mitchie, what's wrong?" He grabbed me from behind and spun me around so I had to face him.

"Dave and Danny want me to move to Colorado with them." I replied. He started laughing but stopped once he realized I was serious.

"Oh, you're serious? You're actually thinking about leaving with them? Mitchie they left you with that asshole, they. . ."

"I know, Chad. B. . . but it really wasn't their fault. They were thirteen and sixteen, they didn't really have any control over what happened to me." He started to walk away, his whole body tense.

"What the hell, Chad? Why are you the one walking away? I'm the one that's going through shit, I'm the one. . ."

"You think that the whole world revolves around you, don't you? That when something goes wrong that poor little McKayla falls apart. Well, newsflash, babe. Not everything is about you." I grabbed his elbow. He turned back around and my eyes immediately went to the lipstick mark on his neck. I let go of his arm and backed away.

"Oh, I'm sorry. I'll let you get back to the bitch that's waiting for you." I said, bitterly. I pulled my hood over my head and started to walk fast.

"God, I sounded jealous." I whispered, wiping my wet cheeks. Could Rae be right? Did I like Chad?

****

"Mitchie!" I blinked in surprise and pulled my ear buds out of my ear. Just as I stood up a rock hit me in the forehead.

"Ouch! What the hell?" I grumbled, looking out my window. I found Chad standing in front of me, nothing but a pair of boxers on.

"What the. . ." I started busting up, clapping my hands.

"Okay, okay. I have got to go get my camera." He grabbed my wrist, not looking even the slightest bit amused.

"Can I come in?" I could feel the smile fall from face in an instantly.

"I guess. My dad's down the hall. . ."

"I know, why do you think I'm coming in through your window?" He mumbled, sliding into my room. He sat in the middle of my bed, running his hands through his hair repeatedly.

"Chad, are you okay?" I whispered, not wanting my dad to hear me talking to someone. I walked over and shut my door, waiting for Chad to respond.

"My family's over." He finally said after a few minutes of silence. I didn't have to ask what he meant by that.

"Your dad is there." He nodded, dropping one of his hands on to my bed.

"T. . . that's not why I don't want to be there." He stuttered, which was really unusual. I had never in my life ever thought about Chad being nervous.

"Chad, are you sure you're okay?" I repeated, sitting on my bed, staring at him worriedly.

"I. . . I can't talk about it." He said.

"Talk about what? Chad, what can't you talk about?" I grabbed his hand, my eyes on his tense back.

"T. . . those lipstick marks weren't from a girl. . . not exactly." He whispered, his breathing starting to quicken.

"Chad. . ." He cut me off.

"My aunt, my dad's sister. She. . . she comes over every few weeks. She. . ." His voice cracked as he turned his face away from me. I could feel the reality of what he had just said setting in.

"Oh, God. Chad." I said, forcing him to look at me. His eyes were glistening in the bright light of my room, he almost looked like he was going to cry.

"She's married. She always has been. B. . . but it never stopped her. She forced me to have sex with her when I was thirteen." I stared at him in horror, my own hands starting to shake along with his.

"That's why. . . is that why you treated me the way you did?" Is that why he was on meds? Because his aunt has been molesting him since he was a kid?

"I shouldn't have. You shouldn't have had to be the one that took everything I was feeling. I used you like some punching bag because I couldn't keep my feelings bottled up and you were just as fucked up as I was. I'm sorry, Mitchie." He touched my cheek, then let his hand slide down to my mouth.

"What the fuck?" I winced internally at the sound of my dad's booming voice. Chad let his hand fall from my cheek as he glared at my dad.

"Get the fuck out of my daughters room!" My dad was about to grab me from behind when Chad flew off the bed and stood in front of me.

"Don't you dare lay a hand on her. The only reason she even tries to stick around is because she can't stop loving you asshole!" He snarled. My dad didn't hesitate to swing at Chad. I really don't think he knew that Chad was a lot stronger then he was, and with him being drunk it made him even weaker.

"Who are you to talk, kid? Is this what you've been doing lately, Mitchie? Have you been messing around with him?" I shook my head, getting ready to stand up. Chad pushed me back on to the bed. They stood their for a moment, Chad and my dad face to face. Then finally my dad lifted his hands up in surrender and walked out of my room, slamming the door as loudly as he could behind him.

"I hate him." Chad stated, glaring at my blue door.

"He's just like my piece of shit dad. Has he ever touched you? Other than that night?" I bowed my head, shaking it.

"Mitchie, you said Danny and David offered you a way out, right?" Chad asked, kneeling down in front of me.

"Yeah."

"Then why don't you take it? Leave this hell hole. If I had a chance, I would leave. You aren't leaving anything behind." I scoffed, staring into his beautiful blue eyes.

"It's not that easy, Chad. I love him, and I don't want to leave him by himself. He'll. . . he'll kill himself. No one will be here to take care of him if he passes out. . ."

"And you shouldn't have to do that! You are a seventeen year old girl, Mitchie. You don't need to be taking care of some worthless excuse for a father. I better get back home before my mom loses it." I followed him to the window, leaning out of it when he was finally in the grass outside.

"You won't tell anyone, right?" He asked.

"Of course not." I replied, a little offended. He took a step forward and leaned in and for a fraction of a second I thought he was about to kiss me. His lips touched my cheek instead.

"I'll see you around, Mac. Remember what I said. Care about yourself before anyone else." He ran into the dark night before I could respond. I shut and locked my window before tossing myself on to my bed and burying my face in the pillow. In that moment I knew to things for sure.

One; I was probably going to say yes to my brothers.

Two; Chad Follet wasn't actually as much of an ass as I thought he was and I. . . I may even be starting to like him.

Chapter 9

Your Star

I made sure I woke up as early as I could the next morning. I slipped out of my house at a quarter to six and caught Chad's Dad and aunt just as they were packing up the car to leave.

"Oh, McKayla! Hello!" Mr. Follet said, closing the trunk. I gave him as fake of a smile as I could before turning to his sister and taking a step closer.

"I actually wanted to talk to Michelle." I said, turning my attention to her. She looked surprised as I took another step toward her. I lifted my hand up and slapped her across the face as hard as I could. She stumbled back in shock.

"You are one sick bitch! The next time you even think about touching Chad, I will make sure you rot in prison. Now get out of here before I change my mind." Her eyes were wide as she scurried into her car and drove off. Mr. Follet stood in front of me, his face pale.

"What? Can. . ." I smacked his hand away. Chad came jogging out of the house, pulling a shirt over his head.

"What happened? Mitchie, are you okay?" The worry was clear in his voice. He stopped in front of his father and me, looking back and forth between us.

"She just hit your aunt. W. . . what did she mean by her touching you, Chad?" Chad turned to me and I swear there was relief in his eyes.

"Nothing, Dad. It doesn't matter. Mitchie needs a ride to school so we better get going. We have something to do today." His dad gave us a weird look before nodding. Chad followed me back to my house.

"What did you do? Did you really hit her?" Chad asked, anxious.

"Yeah. She's fucked in the head for doing that to you, Chad." He nodded in agreement. We stayed quiet as we headed down the street, it was Chad who finally broke the silence.

"Have you. . . are you still a virgin?" He asked. I started coughing to cover up my laugh.

"I. . . that really isn't any of your business, Chad. Why would you even ask that?" I responded, my cheeks flushed.

"I'm just curious. I never got the chance to lose it to someone I cared about. The only woman I've ever. . ." I held my hand up, not wanting him to go on.

"You mean you've never actually slept with a girl your age? All those times at parties and. . ." I trailed off, stopping myself from continuing to walk.

"Yeah. They tried to get me too but I always freaked out and left, telling them to tell everyone we did it." I couldn't hold back my surprise. That means that our famous Bad Boy had never been with a girl.

"Well if it makes you feel any better no one has ever wanted to touch me, let alone sleep with me." I said. He frowned, looking up at my house.

"I don't know why. You're pretty hot. I don't see why anyone would be stupid enough not to ask you out." I could feel heat rush to my cheeks.

"Thanks, Chad." One side of his mouth tugged up into a smile. I started to walk up toward my house when I felt Chad grab my arm and spin me around. I didn't even have a chance to ask what he was doing before his lips touched mine. He pulled me against him, deepening the kiss. My mind took over and my hands wrapped themselves around his neck.

"McKayla!" I jumped, my eyes shooting open as I took a step back.

"I'll be there in a second, Dad!" I yelled. Chad's face was emotionless for a second before he said something.

"I. . . I'll see you later." I bit my lip, nodding as he walked back toward his house.

****

"Mitchie!" I spun around to face Chad, thoughts from this morning starting to resurface.

"Hey, I've been trying to talk to you all day. I need to talk to you." I hugged my books tightly against my chest.

"If this is about this morning. . . I think it was a mistake. I can't. . . we can't. . ." He blinked in surprise.

"No, I wasn't going to ask you about that. I was wondering if you wanted to come to a movie with Louis and I. He's bringing Regan and I really don't want to be a third wheel." It was my turn to be shocked.

"Why didn't they ask me if I wanted to come? I guess they hate me too." I said more to myself than him. He gave me a sad look before tossing his arm over my shoulder.

"Everyone's just jealous that you get to hang out with me. Because you know I'm amazing and so does everyone else." He joked. I didn't laugh as we walked outside of the school.

"Oh come one, Mitchie. Don't make me carry you out to my car and kidnapp you. Laugh, giggle, smile!" He shouted. I slapped his arm, trying to hold back a laugh.

"You're such an idiot." He took it as a compliment and grinned.

"But I'm your idiot so that's all right."

****

"Are you sure it's okay? I mean, Chad's been an ass to you for a long time."

"It's not a date, Danny. We're just hanging out because he doesn't want to be a third wheel."

"Are you sure? It kind of seems like he's trying to pick up on you." I turned around to find my brother staring at me worriedly.

"You worry too much." I mumbled.

"It's my job, Mitchie. I'm your older brother and our worthless father doesn't give a shit. He's scared of Chad." I sighed and sat down on the bed beside him.

"Danny, I'll be fine. We're just going to see a movie. It's harmless." I assured him. He ruffled my curly black hair and stood up.

"Whatever you say, Mac. Now let's go." I hurried out of the room after him and found Chad sitting on the arm of the love seat talking to David.

". . . I doubt it. I could look into it for you though." David finished saying whatever he was talking about. Chad nodded and turned his attention to me. He took in my appearance, smiling.

"You look nice." He held his hand out to me and I took it hesitantly. Danny watched us, his eyes following Chad's every move.

"It was nice seeing you guys again. I'll have her back here once the movies over." Danny was about to respond to Chad but David smacked the back of his head and whispered something to him. Dan mocked him and walked into the kitchen.

"Have fun!" David shouted as Chad shut the door behind us. We walked down to Chad's car and he held the door open for me.

"What were you and Dave talking about?" I asked once he got into the car. He shrugged.

"Nothing important." He said, but I could tell by the look in his eyes that he was hiding something. Most of the drive was quiet, excluding the few comments Chad made about a song on the radio. I opened my mouth in confusion as we drove past the movie theater.

"Chad, what the hell? We just passed the. . ."

"I lied. Rae and Louis never asked me either. I just wanted to take you somewhere and I knew you wouldn't come if I asked you." I stared at him, still confused.

"Chad, my brothers think. . ."

"David knows where I'm taking you, don't worry. Now stop talking before I tape your mouth shut. I'm trying to focus, I don't usually drive around here at night." I rolled my eyes at his immaturity and stared at the window.

"Can you at least tell me where we're going?" I asked.

"Nope. Then it wouldn't be a surprise, would it?" He asked, a mischievous look in his eyes. Oh god, what does he have planned?

Chapter 10

I Wanna

"Why did you bring me to a field in the middle of no where, are you going to kill me?"

"I thought about it, but there wouldn't be any fun in that. David knows where we are." I couldn't stop the laugh from escaping my mouth as he laid the blanket on the ground. He patted the spot beside him once the blanket was laid out.

"Don't you remember when our parents used to bring us out here every holiday? It was always beautiful, especially on the fourth of July." I nodded, recalling the memories.

"I remember the first time I realized that I had a crush on you. We had been here for the fourth and you had been so sad because some little punk pushed you on the slide earlier that day." I turned to him in surprise.

"My sick aunt may have taken my virginity, but you were my first kiss, Mitchie." He added, looking up at the stars above us.

"I don't remember. . ."

"I figured you didn't. Why would you? I was just some messed up kid that liked you." I looked down at the grass, sliding a blade of it between my fingers.

"Chad, I want you to think a little differently of me. Maybe you think your really messed up, but have you seen me? I'm some bi-polar freak that everyone hates, including my best friend." He rolled his eyes.

"You think so lowly of yourself it actually makes me feel bad. You're lucky, Mitchie. You'll find someone you love, you'll give him the one thing you treasure, the one thing you should save for someone you care about." He sounded so bitter it made me cringe.

"Chad, you'll find someone too. You'll love her and you'll marry her and. . ."

"I highly doubt that I'll ever find someone like you, Mitchie. You're the only one that can see through me, that actually cares about how I feel and who I really am." Something came over me in that moment. I grabbed his face and crushed my lips against his. He didn't even hesitate to tangle his hands through my hair.

"Chad, do it." I whispered, tugging at the bottom of his shirt. He pulled away, pushing me forward.

"What?" He asked, his mouth hanging open.

"You said that you won't find someone like me, and I want to lose it to someone I love. And deep down I still remember how close we were when we were kids, Chad. Everyone fucking hates me and I just want to feel loved for a change. Please." I whispered, pulling my own t shirt off. His eyes flashed with more emotions than I could count.

"Are you sure?" He asked, his hands on my waist.

"Yes." I said, before throwing myself back against him. And in that moment as he peeled his own shirt off I did feel some sort of relief. I knew it was wrong, that I was only using him. But I was tired of feeling hated, neglected, and honestly he was the only one that made me feel normal.

*****

I sat in the car, my eyes focused on everything passing by.

"I. . . Mitchie, are you okay?" Chad asked, speaking for the first time in the last hour.

"I'm fine, Chad." I replied. He didn't look like he believed me, but didn't question me either. It was when we pulled down our street that my head whipped up. There were tons of ambulances and cars sitting in front of my house, my dad and brothers no where in sight.

"Mitchie!" I flew out of Chad's car once it came to a stop, ignoring him calling after me. A wave of relief washed over me when I saw David and Danny standing in front of our house.

"Mac!" Danny yelled over the loud sirens. I could feel my heart start racing as another thought crossed my mind. Where was my dad?

"Mac!" Danny was closer now, his eyes dark and emotionless. He was hiding something.

"Dad. . ." I whimpered, backing away. Finally sadness took the place of the cold look in his eyes.

"Dave and I came home, we found him in his bedroom. He left a note and. . ." My eyes darted away from my older brother and to the stretcher that was being brought out of the house. I was about to launch myself toward the paramedics and my dad on the stretcher, when arms wrapped around me from behind.

"Mitchie. Don't." Chad whispered in my ear, pulling me back against him. The realization of everything that was happening started to set in and I started screaming, reaching for my brother.

"Let me go! Chad let me go!" I cried, kicking and screaming. Chad's grip didn't loosen at all.

"Mitchie, screaming and crying isn't going to do you any good. It won't change anything." I tried to elbow him but ended up elbowing the car behind him.

"Fuck you, Chad! Let me go! I want to see my dad! Let me. . ." He slapped a hand over my mouth, his other arm still tight around my waist.

"Is it a good idea?" Chad asked Danny.

"No. He looked... pretty bad when Dave and I found him. I wouldn't let her see him." I started to calm down at my brother's response, tears streaming down my cheeks.

"Do you know what happened?" Chad wondered, probably asking more for me than himself.

"I... I think he finally had it. The note said he thought Mac was going to go with us and that he was the only thing holding her back. He said she would be better off without him." I collapsed against Chad, strange sounds leaving my mouth.

"Mitchie." I ignored Chad and dug my nails into his back as I turned myself around to hug him.

"It's going to be okay."

"Stop lying to me." I whined, glaring up at him. His eyes were just as emotionless as Danny's.

"Okay, you want the truth? I think the piece of shit was selfish for trying to kill himself. What if you had been home? You would have been scared, a horrified. And what if you were going to stay here? He is a worthless piece of crap that honestly doesn't even deserve to live." I winced at his words, his expression softened slightly.

"Dave wants to take her back to the hotel with us." Danny cut in, staring at Chad.

"I mean, she could sleep at my house. My mom loves her." Chad replied.

"I would say that's fine, but there will be cops here all night." I looked back at Chad, waiting for his response.

"Why don't you ask her what she wants?"

"Because she'll end up going to the hospital if she has the chance. The thing we need to worry about is which of us she won't go running out on." The minute it left Danny's mouth, I knew he knew which person I'd pick.

"Dave and are going to stay here for a little while longer, but we'll come by in the morning to pick her up and everything." Danny ripped me from Chad's grip and pulled me into a hug.

"I love you, Mitchie. Dave loves you. Dad even loved . . . loves you." I nodded and watched him walk back up the stairs to the house. Chad wrapped his arms around me, pushing me gently toward the street so we could cross it and go to his house.

"Mitchie. . ."

"I don't want to hear it." I snapped, lacing my fingers through his as we approached his house. He stopped me in front of his door and touched my cheek with his thumb.

"Everything will work itself out, I promise." I so desperately wanted to believe him, even though I knew deep down that my life had just changed dramatically and would never go back to the way it was.

Chapter 11

Falling Apart

I couldn't bring myself to climb out of Chad's bed. I had tossed and turned all night, barely getting any sleep. I was glad that it was the weekend, that seemed to be the only good thing about today.

"Just sleep up here, I'll crash on the couch." Chad had demanded, and I couldn't have been more relieved. I'd slept on my couch at my house more times than I could count and it had been horrible. But as I stared at his popcorn ceiling, counting the bumps, my mind kept drifting back to last night. I had just given my virginity to the bad boy, our school's Mr. Perfect. I honestly didn't know if I regretted it yet or not, I know it was all because I wanted a distraction. And maybe I did regret that, using Chad as my own personal distraction from the horrible reality I'd been living in lately.

"Mitchie! Daniel's on the phone!" I groaned and dragged myself out of the comfortable bed. I jogged down the stairs and found Ms. Follet at the bottom of them. I took the phone from her outstretched hand.

"Hello? Dan?" I yawned, leaning against the wall.

"They have him on life support. Dave thinks that they should just take him off and well, you know. I. . . we wanted to know what you want to do." I almost dropped the phone. Chad walked across the room to stand beside me, staring down at me worriedly.

"Danny. . . they can't. He's only been there for a day, he'll wake up and. . ."

"And then what? Are we just going to let him go back to his old ways, if he wakes up? He's pretty much gone, Mitchie. He did what he did so he would die. Shouldn't we let him have his wish?" I slid down the wall at his words, bringing a shaky hand to my forehead.

"No." I whispered.

"Mitchie, you're being selfish. He wanted to die, so why don't you let him? He didn't want to live in this world anymore. He. . ."

"Shut up!" I cried, finally breaking down. I slammed my head back against the wall over and over, trying to push the thoughts Danny had just put in my head away.

"Mitchie, stop." Chad said quietly, kneeling down. I pushed him away when he tried to grab the phone from my grip.

"Mac, are you okay?" Danny asked, obviously hearing my crying. Chad finally pried the phone from my grip and handed it to his mom. She brought the phone to her ear and walked into the kitchen. Chad moved so that he was directly in front of me, his blue eyes searching mine.

"You have meds, right? Where are they?" I was surprised that he even knew I had them.

"M. . . my purse." I stuttered, pointing at the couch. He grabbed my purse from the couch and searched it.

"Which one do you need? The Bi-polar ones or the Anti-depressants?" He asked, confused as he held the two bottles up. I took one of the bottles from him and tried to get the cap off.

"Mitchie, let me help."

"Leave me alone. I. . . I can do it myself." I said, finally able to open the bottle. He grabbed a water bottle from around the corner in the kitchen and handed it to me. I took the pill and dropped the bottle beside me.

"I hate my life, Chad. I fucking hate it." I snapped, shutting my eyes. I felt him sit down against the wall beside me, his hand resting on my leg.

"Don't say that, Mitchie. Don't be selfish like your dad, please." He pleaded, his voice cracking. I glanced sideways at him and sighed.

"I won't."

****

"You don't have to be such an asshole about it!" Chad growled, pushing Dave away. David laughed sarcastically, shaking his head in amusement.

"Don't tell me you liked him, Chad. Don't tell me that you actually believe the piece of shit has a right to live. You have no idea what he did to my mom, what he did to Danny and me." Chad looked startled for a moment before he snapped back.

"I didn't. The guy was a piece of shit, and I saw him hit her, David. But I'm not thinking about him. I am thinking how Mitchie will feel if he does die. Stop putting your own feelings in front of hers. You didn't spend your whole life caring for the ass, she loves him." Both boys turned to look at me, I only stared back, not moving.

"I don't know what the hell you have to do with any of this. Just because your fucking my sister, it doesn't make you part of this family." David replied, crossing his arms.

"I have everything to do with this, David. I was the one that was here her whole life. I'm the one that saw how she tried to hide that fact that her dad was a piece of shit, how she tried to convince herself other wise. I've been more of a friend, a brother to her then you have." David, to my surprise, took a step back, bowing his head. He looked almost as if he were ashamed.

"You're right. You don't know how many times I fought with Danny on coming back to get her. But I thought she had a great life, I thought she had friends and a boyfriend and. . ."

"No. All she has is me. And if you can't see that she's hanging out to life by a thin thread you must be blind." I watched the two boys, how both of their expressions softened once they brought my life into the equation.

"Mitchie, you okay?" Chad finally asked, holding his hand out to me. I nodded and wrapped my arms around him. In that moment all I wanted was my life to go back to the way it had been a month and a half ago. When Rae would sit with me at my table, talking about how much I was crushing on Louis and how much of an asshole Chad was. When I could go home and talk to my dad without him being hammered.

"McKayla answer me." I recoiled, hearing Chad call me by my real name.

"Obviously I'm not okay, Chad. I just want to go home." I whispered. Dave gave me a sympathetic look.

"You can't. They won't even let Dan in to grab his stuff." I dropped my gaze to the tile floor.

"I know." I said, clinging on to Chad.

"I'm so sorry, Mac. I never wanted anything to. . ."

"Don't apologize, David. No matter how much you apologize, how much I cry, nothing is going to change. Dad's still probably going to die, everyone hates me, and I honestly don't even know if I want to stay here anymore. I just want to escape it all, I want to leave." It was then, for the first time all day, that I saw the boys exchange a look before they both laid a hand on my shoulder.

"We'll support you no matter what your choice is, Mitchie."

Chapter 12

Someday's Gone

I ended up going back to Chad's again. David had said he'd try to get into my house to grab my stuff.

"Are you sure you want to do this?" Chad asked, standing in the doorway of his room.

"Yes, Chad. Everything around me is falling apart. . . I need to start over." I replied, walking over to him. He nodded, his blue eyes filled with understanding. We made small talk as we walked down the stairs and out of the house. Once we were outside, Chad smirked and swung me around so he could kiss me. I smiled into the kiss, my hand resting on his bicep.

"What the. . ." I jumped back at the Regan's voice. I turned to find her standing beside Louis, both of them staring at us in surprise.

"What happened to the whole "Chad is an asshole" thing? I thought you hated him." I glared at the first thing Rae said to me, she hadn't even hello.

"Maybe I secretly liked him and never told you." I said, my eyes flickering to Louis. He smiled sadly, his eyes narrowed at his best friend.

"Are you seriously still on that Mitchie? I said I was sorry, okay? It's a whole other story when I find out that you've been sleeping with Chad Follet. I'm your best friend, you can tell me anything and you didn't. . ."

"You knew about Kim's party, Rae! And you didn't tell me anything! You just let me go and get myself humiliated!" I screamed, my hands clenching into fists.

"Chad did too, Mitchie! But it's okay, right? Because you finally found someone who's as much of a bitch as you are. And because Chad loves little Mitchie when no one else will, he makes your world all better. Fuck you and the fucking horse you rode in on, Mitchie. Everyone was right, you are a stuck up bitch!" She growled, Louis had to hold her back so she wouldn't move any closer to me. I threw my hands up in the air, tears burning my eyes as I stared at her.

"Go ahead and say anything you want, Regan. I am so done with everyone, with everything. Yeah, maybe I was a bitch, but did you ever stop and wonder why? Did you know I had to go home to my dad hammered every other night? Did you know that I take antidepressants and Bi-polar depression pills? Did you know that my mom is in a fucking crazy house and that's probably where I'll end up too?"

She stood staring at me in horror, both boys looked like it was news to them as well.

"I'm just a crazy bitch like my mom, right? Goodbye, Regan." I walked past her, not even looking to see any of their reactions.

****

I could feel my nails digging into my scalp as I buried my face in my knees.

"We're leaving, Mitchie. Come on." Danny said softly, helping me up. I stopped in front of the mini-van, scanning my surroundings for Chad. He was no where in sight, which honestly didn't surprise me. Not anymore.

"Come on." Danny gave me a slight push and I sighed and climbed into the car, forcing myself to smile. I was finally leaving this hell hole, I should be happy. But deep down, in the pit of my stomach I didn't want to leave and I didn't know why.

****

I set my bag on the floor beside the empty bed. Yawning, I grabbed my laptop out of it and sat in the middle of my bed. I did the stupid thing then, I logged on to The Lover's advice column and stared at it for a moment. He had answered tons of questions within the last hour, which kind of made me sad. He had taken the time to do that but hadn't come to say goodbye to me.

"He doesn't matter anymore, Mitchie. He's in the past and you left that behind." I whispered to myself, but my eyes drifted to the jacket draped across the back of the computer chair. I took a deep breath, an idea starting to come to mind. Maybe there was a way I could have closure, a way for me to leave it all behind for good. I sighed as I clicked on the link to post my own question for Chad. My fingers danced across the keyboard as I wrote what was on my mind.

Dear Lover,

Have you ever felt like the whole world was against you? Have you ever felt like every little thing you did was wrong? Have you ever. . . had feelings for someone you shouldn't? I'm guessing you probably haven't, that you aren't nearly as screwed up as I am. In the last month my life has slowly gone down hill and I really don't know what I did to deserve this. Why did my life have to fall apart? Can you answer me, Lover? Or are you just some person hiding behind a facade because they are to scared to look at themselves in the mirror? Isn't that what everyone's problem is? They can't actually face who they are on the inside so they judge and project themselves on to other people. Any person that believes that you are any better than us is wrong. You are just like us, but have found another way to escape. And I would love for you to be able to show me how you escaped so easily. I doubt that I'll hear back from you, Lover. But you just need to know that not everyone believes the little front you put up. Anonymous

My finger hovered over the Enter key for a few minutes as I stared at what I wrote. Finally I slammed my finger down on it and watched it get put up. I shut my laptop a few minutes afterward and walked out of the room and to the kitchen. I found Dave and Danny sitting at it, talking. They both smiled when I walked in.

"How is Dad?" I asked, earning a grimace out of both of them.

"Not much better than he was yesterday." David finally said.

"I want to see Mom." I whispered. Danny stood up quickly, his knee slamming against the table.

"Absolutely not. Why in the world would you want to do that?"

"Because I want to see what I have a chance of becoming. Please, Danny." I begged. He looked at our older brother, his eyebrows knitted. David glanced up at me and nodded.

"If she wants to see her, let her. We'll take you to visit her tomorrow." David said. I gave him a thankful smile and was surprised when Danny grabbed the keys and handed me my-Chad's- jacket.

"We are going to go get Ice Cream." I smiled at my brother's back as we walked out of the house. Maybe starting over wouldn't be so bad.

Chapter 13

Here I Sit

"Mom? Hey." David said loudly, kneeling down in front of the middle aged woman. She turned to her son slowly, her lips parting. I took a step back, my heart racing. This wasn't the black haired and blue eyed woman I remembered. Her hair was almost all gray and her eyes were lifeless, dull, and had bright red.

"Mom, it's me Dave." He said quietly, gripping her hand. Her hand started shaking as she stared at him.

"David. What are you doing here?" She asked, smiling. Danny squeezed my hand and pulled me forward.

"Someone wanted to visit you. Mom, this is McKayla." My mom's expression darkened at the mention of my name. She rose out of the chair she was in, glaring at David.

"Why would you bring her here? I told you. . ."

"Dad's on life support. Mac's living with us now. Don't be a bitch, Mom."Danny growled. She turned her attention back to me, taking in my appearance.

"Who's jacket is that?" She asked, gesturing toward Chad's sweatshirt.

"I. . . my. . ."

"Her boyfriend's." David cut in, saving me. I thanked him.

"Well where is he at? Why is she not living with him?" My mom asked my brothers.

"She's seventeen, Mom. She can't. . ."

"I had you at seventeen, Dave. She could get pregnant. I bet she's some whore already." She snapped, cut down after cut down. I flipped around and started to walk away.

"Why did you really come, McKayla?" My mom called after me, speaking directly to me for the first time.

"I came to see what I had a chance of becoming." I replied. She frowned, tapping her fingers against her arm.

"And did you come to any realizations?" She asked.

"Yeah," I laughed coldly, "I know that I will never become you."

*****

"Wow, he actually responded." I gasped, clicking to open Chad's response to my message. My heart was beating against my chest, my hands shaking nervously. Why was I so nervous?

Dear Anonymous,

Yes. Yes. And Yes. All I can say on the note of having feelings for someone you shouldn't is to try and talk to them, to see if the feelings are mutual. Love is one of the strongest emotions. I can guarantee you that I am just as or more messed up than you are. To be completely honest with you, I probably am exactly what you think I am. A fake. A freak. A loser. I really wish I could answer you, I wish I could tell you I'm sorry. But would it make a difference? And yeah, for those people that do put me on a pedestal, stop. I am no better then you or your friend or your brother. I am just a normal person like you that has had their fair share of heartbreak. My only advice to you, well, keep your head held high. I know it may seem hard sometimes, maybe even impossible, but it isn't. I promise that there is someone out their that loves you. Goodluck. The Lover

"Dammit, Chad." I mumbled to myself. I hadn't actually expected him to reply and his reply had been amazing. He obviously knew that it was me that had sent it up.

"What?" I said when my phone started ringing. I picked it up and brought it to my ear without checking the number.

"Hello?"

"Mitchie?" I laughed at the sound of Chad's voice, he sounded as if someone was holding his nose.

"Yeah? How'd you get my number?" I asked.

"Dave gave it to me. I need to see you, face to face. Can you give me your Skype user name?" I hesitated before giving him all of my information and getting on to it myself. After a few minutes I was greeted by a very beat up looking Chad.

"Jeez! What happened to you?" I gasped, touching my own nose. He looked as if he'd just been jumped. His right eye was swollen shut, a white bandage was across his red nose an his lips were bright red with blood and chapped.

"Peter and Louis happened." He replied, I frowned.

"You have to be more specific, Chad. What did you do?"

"Why is it always something that I did? All I was doing was trying to defend you. Peter's bitch ass couldn't handle it and I guess Louis was in a fighting mood." I stared in shock, my hand moving up to cover my mouth.

"Oh god, Chad. I'm so sorry. You didn't have to defend me. . ."

"Of course I did. You aren't here to defend yourself so I had too. Looks like I'm friendless too. What a fucked up couple we are." The way he said couple made my stomach flutter.

"Chad about the letter I sent you ear. . ."

"You don't have to exaplin. I. . . actually that's what I wanted to talk about. I don't want to be The Lover anymore. I. . . I think I'm going to reveal myself at Prom."

"Are you sure?" He nodded, sighing and then wincing.

"Yeah, I'm done with it. I. . . actually David got me a job over there." I blinked in surprise, my mouth opening.

"Oh." Was my brilliant response.

"My mom said she'd love for me to go to the college over there, she says she wants me as far away from Michelle as possible."

"Oh." I repeated, wanting to slap myself.

"Uh, yeah. Danny said I could stay with you guys. I mean, if that's okay with you." I nodded, not knowing what to say.

"I went to visit my mom today." I stated. His sad expression suddenly grew curious.

"Oh, how was it?" He replied.

"Horrible. But I did learn something pretty great." He cocked his head to the side.

"And what was that?"

"I learned that she is a crazy, judgmental bitch and that I'll never be like her." The curious expression stayed on his face.

"Is that a good thing or a bad thing?"

"Good." I muttered, laying back on my bed and setting the laptop on my knees.

"I never thought I'd say it. . . but I kind of wish you were back here, Mitchie. I miss you." I smiled, feeling my cheeks warm up.

"I miss you too, Chad. I better go eat, I'll talk to you later or tomorrow." He nodded and just as I was about to shut my laptop he held up his hand to stop me.

"And Mitchie?"

"Yeah?"

"I just wanted to let you know that I think I may have feelings for someone I shouldn't." He whispered, then the screen went black.

Chapter 14

Don't Leave Me

David and Danny tried to force me to go to school for the next few weeks, I refused. I kept pushing them away or screaming. I didn't even want to get out of bed anymore, I felt paralyzed. It wasn't until the middle of June that I dragged myself out of bed to answer the door since no one was home.

"Hold on a minute!" I yelled, surprised at how normal my voice sounded. I opened the door to find a giant teddy bear.

"What is that?" I asked, a smile tugging at my lips. The person holding the bear walked into the house and laid it against the loveseat. He leaned forward a kissed the smile right off of my lips.

"I thought he would cheer you up. Since I'm a beary nice guy, I figured I'd buy him for you." I frowned, glancing at the giant teddy bear, the back at Chad.

"That was a horrible pun." I said. He took my face between his fingers.

"But it made you smile and that's what matters." He kissed me again, pulling me against him.

"You just show up out of the blue and expect me to run back into your arms? Chad, you've ignored me for three months. Do you know how useless I felt, how alone?" I asked, looking up into his blue eyes. He sighed.

"I had a lot on my mind. I didn't want all of my depression to rub off on you. I know it was no excuse to ignore you, to not. . ."

"You're right, it wasn't." I snapped, cutting him off. His eyes grew dark.

"Do you want me to leave?" He growled. I didn't move or say a word. He flipped around and walked back toward the door.

"Don't leave me." I finally whimpered. He stopped in front of the door, his back tense.

"Say it again." He demanded, his voice cracking.

"Don't leave me, Chad. I need you." I repeated, biting my lip. He stalked back toward me and pushed me back against the wall, his lips crashing into mine. I wrapped my arms around his neck, my heart racing.

"I need you too." He whispered in my ear before lifting me up and carrying me back to my room.

*****

"Mitchie?" Chad breathed out, his finger still trailing my stomach. I lifted my head so I could look at him.

"Yeah?" I said just as quietly.

"My aunt was arrested yesterday." He whispered. I stared in shock.

"What? That's great, Chad. You. . . you aren't happy?" It came out as more of a question then a statement.

"I am. I. . . it's just tearing my family apart more then it already is. I know I'm no one to talk about family right now, I know your hurting more. . ."

"No, Chad. I want to hear what's going on in your life. I don't want you to keep everything bottled up." I replied, resting my head back on his bare chest.

"Come to Prom with me." He whispered, his face buried against my hair.

"I can't, Chad. I'm not going back there and getting humiliated all over again. I. . ."

"That's why you need to go back, Mitchie. Let them know that you're still strong, let them know that you aren't a weak little girl. What happened to my Mitchie? The girl that would bite someone's head off just for calling Regan fat? Or the girl that smiled and laughed even though she was dying inside, just so no one knew they were effecting her." I laughed bitterly.

"She's been gone for a while now, Chad."

"I want her back. I want you to go to prom with me. Please, Mitchie." He pleaded, pushing my head off his chest so he could look me in the eyes.

"Please." He said again. I let out a sigh of defeat, my eyes dropping back toward the blue comforter on top of us.

"Fine. But if they say one word I'm walking out." I replied. He smiled, a genuine smile.

"Thank you." I stuck my tongue out at him childishly and yawned before laying my head back down.

****

"It's not much of a job. It's just painting houses and maybe building a few occasionally." David told Chad, stabbing his fork into his steak. Chad smiled at my brother, nodding.

"That's fine, man. Anything is better than nothing." David nodded in agreement. Danny sent me a weird glance, it had been something he'd been doing all night.

"What is it? Why do you keep looking at me like that?" I finally snapped. He blinked in surprise and spoke.

"You and Chad are together, right?" Chad and I exchanged a look before nodding.

"Yeah. Why?"

"Because he better make sure he doesn't hurt you or I'll bash his brains in." He replied, glaring at Chad. I glanced back down at my food, my stomach churning again. My stomach had it and I darted down the hall and toward the bathroom, puking up the little I had eaten. I laid my head against the bowl, flushing the toilet.

"Mitchie?" I looked up to find Danny standing in the doorway, his arms crossed over his chest as he stared down at me.

"Hmm?" I answered.

"Are you pregnant?"

"Excuse me?" I snapped, dropping my hands from the toilet.

"Did you ever think that's why you've been so bitchy and moody lately?Or why you won't touch your food? And I know you don't have any. . . woman necessities and you haven't asked Dave and I for any for like two months." My breath caught in my throat. I stared at my older brother in horror, realization starting to sink in.

"Danny. . ."

"I know, Mitchie. I'm guessing it was an accident, that Chad probably didn't use protection." I wrapped my arms around myself, shaking my head over and over.

"No, Danny. I. . . no. That means I'm turning into her, I'll become her. I . . ." My brother made a face and walked over to where I was laying against the bath tub. He fell on to the ground beside me, ruffling my hair.

"You won't ever become her, Mitchie. I know you won't. You're way too smart, to nice. And you know there is a huge difference between the two of you. You actually care about other people and how they feel. Mom was a self centered, selfish bitch that only gave a shit about herself." I laid my head against my brother's chest, shutting my eyes.

"I'm scared." I whispered. I couldn't have a baby, I was only seventeen. I still had my whole life a head of me. And what about Chad? I couldn't have him stay with me, waste his whole life because of a mistake we made. He'd be terrified, probably just as scared as I am.

"You're scared? How do you think poor Chad's going to feel?"

"I think he's gonna leave. That he won't want anything to do with us. He's hot, Danny. He can get whatever girl he wants." My brother laughed, I looked up at him in surprise.

"I highly doubt that Chad is going to leave you. Yeah he's a good looking kid, but he's pretty fucked up, Mitchie. I don't know what's wrong with him, but you seem like the only person that calms him down. You should see the way that lovesick puppy looks at you." He replied, smirking. I blushed, laughing quietly.

"I don't think he looks. . ."

"That's because you are a naive little monkey." I rolled my eyes at the nickname.

"Mitchie? Hey, are you okay?" Danny and I both looked toward the door.

"I'm fine, Chad." I assured him. He looked back and forth between Danny and me, than held his hand out to me.

"I'm exhausted, and you look like crap. Let's go to bed." I took his hand, giving him a playful glare.

"You make me feel so beautiful, Chad." He grinned, throwing his arm over my shoulder.

"I try, babe. I try."

Chapter 15

Can't Take It

I dropped the third test back into the sink, slamming my head back against the door frame. I took a deep breath before walking back into my room and pulling my shirt up. My mouth went dry. I could see the bump that was starting to form, and my hands slowly slid to touch it.

"Mitchie?" I dropped my shirt and spun around to face Chad. He had started to work a couple days ago and had fallen asleep instantly every time his head had hit the pillow. I hadn't had a chance to even speak with him all week, and honestly I was kind of glad. But today he had noticed that my stomach issues weren't just some flu and he had started to get worried.

"Hi." I mumbled, waving my hand shyly. He didn't say a word and I understood when my eyes went to the white test in his hand.

"Chad. . ."

"Mitchie, tell me this is Destiny's. Please." He whispered, but his eyes told me he already understood.

"I. . . I'm so sorry, Chad. You don't have to stay, you can leave. I. . . I would understand. I'm some crazy. . ."

"Calm down, Mac. It's okay." He responded, setting the test on my dresser before pulling me into a hug.

"I'm turning into her already, Chad. I. . . I can't." I whimpered, my nails digging into his back through his tank top.

"Stop, Mitchie. You won't become her. Just like I'll never become my dad."

"What if I leave it, Chad? What if I can't handle a child, what if I just make the same mistakes that she did?" I asked, my whole body shaking.

"Then we'll give it up for adoption, Mitchie. If you don't think your ready, if you're scared that you'll leave her, then give it up. Let it have a normal life." I shook my head.

"I'm scared, Chad. I'm so scared." He pushed me away from him, his eyes dark and glistening in the dim light of the room.

"I'm here for you, Mitchie. I support whatever you want to do." I laid my head against his chest, wishing everything would just end.

*****

I leaned against the wall, staring as my mom rocked back and forth in her rocking chair, Ellie on her lap. David and Destiny sat across from them, smiling and laughing.

"Hey, Mac." Chad whispered, wrapping his arms around me from behind. I relaxed against him, my eyes still burning.

"How could she be like that? How could she push me away, throw me to the side, but love Ellie the way she does? What did I do wrong?" I asked, not looking at him. He sighed, his chin resting on my shoulder.

"You didn't do anything, Mitchie. Stop blaming yourself. And if you don't believe me then come on." He took my hand in his own and dragged me over to my family. Dave's smile dropped and Destiny looked worried.

"Auntie Mitchie!" Ellie yelled, wrapping her arms around my legs. I ruffled her hair, trying to smile. My mom's eyes went to my stomach, even though it was covered up by one of Chad's sweatshirts.

"McKayla." She said, her voice cold. Chad gave her a fake smile, wrapping his arm around my waist.

"Ms. Halley, it's nice to see you again." He said, holding his free hand out to her. She frowned, confused.

"Do I know you?"

"It's me, ma'am. Chad." He told her, smiling. Her eyes widened.

"Oh, Chad! Look how much you've grown!" She exclaimed, trying to pull him toward her. He stayed right beside me, his eyes narrowing at her.

"Yeah. It's been like ten years," He said bitterly, "I was actually just here for my girlfriend. She has a question for you."

"Girlfriend?" My mom asked, ignoring anything else he had said.

"Yeah. Mitchie, why don't you ask her what you need to so we can go." Chad said, kissing my cheek. I fiddled with the string on the sweatshirt, not looking at my mom as I asked the question.

"What did I do? Why'd you leave me?" I croaked out. For a second I thought I saw guilt flash through her eyes. Finally she took a deep breath and gestured toward the seat beside her.

"Sit down, McKayla." She whispered. I looked over at Chad who nodded and walked around to stand behind my chair, his hands on my shoulders.

"I was terrified when I found out I was having a girl, McKayla. I lost it. I did drugs, I drank. I. . . I stopped caring. Because of what happened to me as a child. I was molested by my Uncle until I left for college, and I always thought that if I had a girl that some sick piece of shit would do the same thing." She stopped, turning to face me.

"You're dad was excited, so were Dave and Dan. They loved the thought of having a little sister and a daughter. B. . . but I was scared. I didn't want you to become me, McKayla. Some messed up alcoholic and druggie, a bi-polar freak. I also knew, since Dave and Dan came out okay, that you were probably be the problem child. The one that got my problems. Now look at you, your following in my footsteps."

I felt Chad's grip tighten on my shoulder, I could hear his breathing get heavier as well.

"I think we should go." He whispered. I tilted my head back so I could look at him. His blue eyes were dilated and his face looked ashen.

"Nic. . ." I started to say, seeing how weird he was acting. He held up his hand before walking fast out of the room. Dave, Destiny, and my mom all stared after him worriedly.

"What was that about?" Dave asked.

"Nothing. I'll go check on him." I replied after clearing my throat. I hurried out of the room to find Chad standing outside, his forehead pressed against the wall in the hallway.

"Go away." He said quietly.

"Chad, what's. . ."

"I said go away, McKayla!" He yelled, slamming his fist against the wall. I jumped back, my heart racing and my eyes wide with fear.

"Go!" He yelled again. I backed away, before taking off and running out of the hospital, tears streaming down my cheeks. I sat on the curb, wrapping my arms around myself.

"You're following in my footsteps." My mom's voice rang through my head. I let out a cry, shaking my head to get rid of the thoughts.

You can't do this to youself, Mitchie. It's not just you anymore. You have a baby, and crying isn't going to do anything but hurt you both.

You have to make sure you're stronger when the baby comes. You can't fall apart like this, you can't lose it or breakdown. You. . ."

"Mac, I'm so sorry." I ignored Chad, staring at the park across the street from us. At the family that sat under a tree laughing.

"Mac, please. I want to go." I pushed my hair out of my eyes and gave him a sidways glance.

"We can't do this anymore, Chad. We can't breakdown or fall apart. We have another person being brought into our life. We. . ." He sat down on the sidewalk beside me, pulling me against him.

"I know, Mitchie. I know. I. . . I'll do my best. I'm just as scared as you are." I nodded, sniffling. Slowly I lifted my head and we both stared at the family across the street, at the mother and father and how they laughed at the two kids in front of them.

"I want a family like that." I whispered. Chad chuckled, kissing my neck.

"That's great, because I do too."

Chapter 16

Time Stands Still

I watched Chad fix his tie, my eyes traveling down his body.

"You like what you see?" He asked, wiggling his eyebrows suggestively. I smirked, wrapping my arms around his neck.

"I do." I admitted.

"Well, sorry to disappoint you but we have somewhere to be. You'll have me to yourself all night." He kissed me before heading out into the living room. I sighed and pried myself from the wall, following him.

"Oh! You two look wonderful!" Ms. Follet said, grinning. I thanked her, bowing my head.

"Now, you two are going to include me on naming the baby right."

"Yeah, Mom. Sure." Chad mumbled, grabbing my jacket from the coat rack. We had told Mrs. Follet the moment we got here. We knew she would figure out anyway, with only one look at my stomach she would freak out. To our surprise, she didn't get mad or give us "The talk".

"Let me take a picture." We posed for her, Chad yawning afterward.

"You two have fun." She called after us. Chad rolled his eyes, grabbing my waist and pulling me against him.

"Sure."

****

"Oh my god! Bitchie came back!"

"Why is she with Chad?"

"Wow." I tried to ignore the comments, but winced every time one was said. Chad noticed and smiled reassuringly at me, squeezing my hand.

"Don't listen to them. Everything will be fine." As if to prove his point, he kissed me in front of everyone. I heard a few gasps and a few whispers, but forced myself not to care.

"Okay, who missed me?" Chad yelled, walking away from me. I bowed my head as everyone cheered and chanted his name.

"Where have you been, man?" One of the jocks yelled.

"With my girl, Jes!" Chad yelled back. I could feel my cheeks heat up as the whole room turned to me.

"Anyway, I actually have something to tell you guys." Chad said, stepping up on to the stage.

"Hi." My head whipped up at the sound of my best. . . ex best friends voice.

"Hey." I muttered, hoping she would get the hint and leave. She didn't, instead she stood behind me. I glanced back to find that Louis was also behind me, his arm wrapped around her waist.

". . . here goes nothing. Every single one of you has written a letter to The Lover. Don't try to deny it. You guys are probably wondering how I know this." The crowd erupted in whispers.

"Well, I know this because I am the Lover." I heard a bunch of people gasp around me, then they all started yelling.

"Bullshit!"

"Prove it!"

"Yeah!" Chad's eyes met mine and I gave him sympathetic look. He rubbed his forehead, sighing.

"All right. Kailin, you are afraid of going home every night because of your stalker ex boyfriend that won't leave you alone." He pointed at the sophomore, his eyes narrowed.

"Kim, you're afraid you have an STD that you got from one of your father's friends at a Poker match." Chad didn't even try to cover up the story. He continued without hesitation.

"Louis Yeller, you felt bad for leading Mitchie on then going out with her best friend," Chad walked down the steps, the microphone in his hand as he made his way toward his best friend.

"Then you wrote me again asking what you should do about our friendship. You said you felt horrible but didn't know how to apologize. All I have to say to that is fuck you. All of you guys. You put me up on a pedestal, thinking that I was better than all of you. I'm not. I'm just as messed up as every single person in this room. You guys need to accept that. You all should look at yourself, look at what's wrong with you and try to fix it. Although sometimes flaws are what makes us human." I stared at Chad, my eyes wide. When had he become so philosophical?

"Or maybe you can find someone to help you through it all." Chad took my hand in his, kissing the top of it.

"That's all I have to say." He finished, holding the microphone out to one of the teachers.

"Let's get out of here before a riot starts." He whispered in my ear before we headed toward the school exit.

****

"Emilia Rose Follet." Chad said, pushing the shake back toward me. I smiled at the name.

"Rose after your mom?" I guessed. He nodded as he crossed his arms on the table.

"I was thinking Jackson Chad Follet." He raised an eyebrow, his mouth pulling into a smile.

"Jackson after your dad?" He asked. I grinned, pushing the shake back to him.

"Yeah. And Chad after his daddy." I said, sticking my tongue out.

"I think that's a very good name." I rolled my eyes but was interrupted before I could speak.

"Chad Follet? You are under arrested for assault and battery." My eyes grew wide as the cop ripped Chad from the table and shoved him against it, handcuffing him.

"Chad? Hey, you must have the wrong person. . ."

"I'm sorry, Ma'am. I know this may all be a surprise to you but. . . Chad here is under arrest for the assault of Michelle Follet." My jaw fell to the floor as I wrapped my arms around me, feeling sick to my stomach.

"No, sir. You don't understand. She molested him, she's sick and. . ."

"That doesn't give him any right to hurt her." My eyes drifted to Chad.

"Did you . . ."

"I didn't. Go back to my house and tell my mom to meet me at the station. I promise I didn't do it, Mitchie. . ." He was dragged away before I could respond. I grabbed the keys on the table with shaky hands and rushed out of the diner, leaving no trace that we were ever there.

Chapter 17

The Wind Blows

"I wonder if you're a boy or a girl." I whispered to myself, rubbing my stomach. A few people in the room gave me a weird glance, which only earned them a nasty look out of me.

"I told you to get my. . ."

"I have money too, Chad. I didn't want her to be disappointed. They can't keep you in here if they don't have evidence." I snapped, cutting him off. He sighed, running a hand through his short hair as he walked over to me. I could feel all the anxiety and worry slip out of me the minute he pulled me into his warm embrace.

"Thanks, Mac." He breathed into my ear. I laid my head over his heart.

"I love you." I whispered, afraid to look up to see his expression. To my surprise he didn't say anything. He pulled me against him and we walked out of the police station in silence.

****

"Do you want to know the gender?" I snorted, shaking my head Mrs. Follet.

"No. I think it'll be better for it to be a surprise. Right, Chad?" I glanced over at him. He had been silent all night, only speaking when his mother asked him something. He gave me a forced smile and nodded.

"Yeah. I think that's a great idea." Even as he said it, I could tell he was still distant.

"Do you have a name for it if it's either gender?"

"Emilia Rose and Jackson Chad." I answered automatically. Her eyes started to glisten, but Chad cleared his throat before a word could be said.

"I'm exhausted, I think I'll go to bed early tonight." He kissed his mom's cheek, then leaned down to kiss me. I grabbed his arm as he pulled away.

"Are you okay?" I asked. He smiled, but it didn't meet his eyes.

"I'm fine, babe." He kissed me lightly again before turning around and jogging up the stairs. I frowned as I turned back to his mom.

"Is he all right?" She questioned, still looking at the stairs.

"I think he's just tired." I replied.

"Are you keeping it? The baby?" She snapped, catching me by surprise.

"Excuse me?" I gasped, glaring at her.

"It's my grandchild, I have a right to know." She growled, her expression and voice completely changing.

"I don't think it's any of your business." I said just as coldly.

"It's my business if I don't want some bi-polar little girl raising my goddamn grandchild! Or are you just going to leave it when he or she will need you the most?" I recoiled, nearly falling out of my chair.

"I don't think that you are a fit mother, McKayla. You. . ."

"Listen, bitch. This is my child! Not yours! Yes, it may be Chad's, but it is between me and your son. Not you! And if you ever," I paused, pointing my finger at her angrily, "say I'm like my mother again, you will never see your grandchild." I stormed out of the house before she could reply, letting the door slam loudly behind me.

*****

"I'll be a good mom, I promise. I'll stay with you and I won't ever let anyone hurt you." I said, wiping a stray tear from my cheek.

"Mitchie?" I recognized the voice, but didn't care enough to try and place it.

"Go away." I mumbled, laying both of my hands back on my stomach.

"Mitchie, it's freezing out here. What are you doing?" I looked up to meet familiar green eyes.

"Go away, Louis." I repeated. He shook his head, his mouth opening.

"I came here to talk to Chad, not to find you freezing to death." He said.

"Louis I. . . ah!" A sharp pain shot through my stomach. Louis kneeled, his eyes wide.

"Are you okay? Mitchie?" I shook my head as another sharp pain shot through me. I let out another cry. I grabbed on to the collar of his shirt, gasping.

"Chad. Call Chad." I screamed again, my hands digging into my palms. Louis dialed Chad's number quickly and spoke into the phone. He dropped his phone on to the black top once he ended the call.

"Mitchie? Hey, why do you look so pale?" He asked, his hands on my stomach. I couldn't see his face anymore, black spots had started to appear and everything around me had begun to spin.

"The baby." I whimpered. He blinked, his green eyes lit with fear.

"Baby? Mitchie what baby?" I fell forward into his arms before I could reply and everything around me went black.

Chapter 18

Affection

I woke up to beeping. It wasn't an alarm clock kind of beeping, it was almost as if it were going along with my heart. . .

"Mitchie? Are you awake?" I opened my eyes only to shut them quickly. Slowly I tried to open them again and was able to make out Chad's figure leaning over me.

"The baby?" I croaked. He smiled, touching my cheek.

"Babies." He corrected. My half open eyes grew wide.

"What?" I whispered.

"You went through to much stress a couple days ago, Mitchie. You were having a panic attack. The babies were feeling it and they started to kick." He kissed my hand, his blue eyes dancing with relief.

"You keep saying babies." I stated. He laughed, grinning.

"The doctor found another baby," He poked my stomach, "He said the last time you were here it was too early to tell." I could feel horror starting to build in my chest.

"Twins?" I clarified. He nodded, his smile starting to fade when he saw the look on my face.

"Mitchie, it'll be fine. We can take care of them. . ."

"What about school, Chad? And neither of us have a steady job. How are we supposed to support two kids?" I asked. He looked away, almost ashamed.

"I already told Dave and Danny, they said that they'll help us out. And I'm trying to get a better job." I reached out to run my hand down his cheek, he laid his own over mine.

"I'm sorry about my mom. I only caught the last of what she said. I. . . I can't believe she would even says something like that." I shook my head, not wanting to talk about it.

"I'm hungry." I muttered. He smirked and laid both of his hands on my stomach.

"I bet you guys are. I'll let the doctor know you're up." He kissed me before jogging out of the room. As I stared after him a smile tugged at my lips. He seemed so excited, so happy about the news. Well, at least one of us isn't scared to death.

*****

"Do you need anything? A blanket? Food? A. . ." I held my hand up, yawning.

"No, all I want right now is you, Chad." He rolled his eyes and fell on to the couch beside me.

"I'm sorry. I'm just trying to get the hang of this New Dad thing." He laid his head against my shoulder, staring up at me.

"I know, Nic. But you don't have to worry about me. I can take care of myself." He rubbed his hand along my stomach.

"Tell me that in a few months when you can barely walk." He winked, sliding his hand up my shirt. I pushed him away, biting my lip.

"No, Chad." He pouted but listened and reached for the remote on the table.

"What if they are both girls? Oh, God. I can't deal with both of my girls dating assholes like me." He looked horrified at the realization.

"Or they could both be boys and turn out to be assholes like you." I pointed out, laughing. He glared at me.

"Nope. Stop laughing. I'm being serious, here. I think we should find out the genders, Mitchie. I want to prepare myself." I sighed, thinking about what he said. I shrugged it off and tried to change the subject.

"Louis? Did you guys make up or?"

"Yeah. He apologized, then freaked out when he found out I got you pregnant. He has a pretty great right hook." He gestured toward his bandaged nose.

"Do you think he'll tell Rea?" I asked. He shrugged, flipping through the channels.

"Probably. Why does it matter? We aren't in Cali anymore, Mac. Everyone there hates me now anyway." It was his turn to yawn. He stopped on some crime drama and moved so that he was laying down. I stared at him, watching as his breathing got heavier and he fell asleep. I shook myself out of my creep moment and stood up to go to the kitchen.

"Why am I doing this?" I asked myself, picking up my phone. I hit the contact and listened to it ring for a moment.

"Hello?"

"Dave? I need you to come pick me up."

*****

"Adoption agency? Mitchie, are you sure?" I shook my head, my eyes starting to burn.

"What if I can't support them, Dave? What if Chad can't? S. . . shouldn't they be able to have a good life?" My brother thought about what I said for a second before gripping my shoulders and staring down into my eyes.

"Sometimes money doesn't matter, McKayla. Your children, they'll love you and Chad no matter what. They won't care if you don't have money as long as you keep a roof over their head and love them. I know you, Mac. You won't be able to do it, give them up. Deep down you want to be better than mom, and that's something mom would do." I threw my arms around my brother and started bawling. I couldn't take it anymore. Maybe it was the hormones, maybe it was the guilt I felt for even coming here.

"Take me back to Dan's." I whispered. Dave smiled knowingly.

"Of course."

***

"How could you? Dammit, Mitchie! Tell me, talk to me! Don't go and do stupid shit like that." Chad yelled for the hundreth time. I winced, looking down at the tile.

"You said you supported whatever I wanted to do." I said quietly. Chad grabbed my shoulders, glaring at me.

"Don't feed me that bullshit. You don't want to give them up! You are only letting what my mom said worm it's way into your brain. I love you, McKayla. I fucking love you and I hate seeing you broken and hurt and scared. I try to be strong but when I see you doing stupid shit like what you just did, it makes me lose it." I stared up at him in shock. He. . . he had just said he loved me. But didn't I already know that?

"I knew when I was eight, eight! I knew that I loved you. And then I went and ruined everything, I never thought you would forgive me. These babies, Mitchie, they are my godsend. You are." He took my face in his hands and kissed me. It wasn't rough or gentle, but somewhere in between. It was passionate, it was his way of proving that he loved me.

"I want to keep them. I do, Chad." I cried, burying my face against him. He held on to me, whispering in my ear.

"I know, Mac. And everything will be okay. We'll be good parents."

"Chad, I want to know. I want to know the sexes too." He smiled, kissing my forehead.

"It'll be okay, I promise." And god, I really hope he's right.

Chapter 19

Why Worry?

The next three months went by in a blur. It was full of paint, toys, and building things. Chad hadn't been wrong, I could barely walk now. Somehow Chad had been able to manage working on the nursery and working two jobs. Even against my wishes, he wouldn't quit either of his jobs.

"We get to find out the sexes today." Chad said, laying a teddy bear in one of the cribs.

"Yeah." I muttered. He frowned, his eyes searching mine.

"You're scared." It wasn't a question.

"Of course I am, Chad. I'm even more worried about having them." I sat down in the rocking chair, laying my head back against the pillow behind me.

"Mitchie," He whispered, walking over to me, "everything will be okay. You'll be ready, I know you will." He leaned against the wall to my right.

"And what am I supposed to tell them when they are old enough to know about their grandparents? Oh, you know. Your grandmother's are both bitches, one of your grandfather's is on life support, and the other is in jail. What a great family we are!" I exclaimed sarcastically. Chad didn't say anything, he only stared down at me, his face emotionless.

"My mom isn't a bitch, Mac. She only cares about the well-being of her grandchildren." I glared up at him, shaking my head.

"So now you want to defend her? After what she said to me? After making me have a panic attack? Chad, you can't. . ."

"Can't what? I can't keep in contact with my mother? I have to choose between you and her?"

"Yes. Chad, I can't deal with her. I already have enough issues with my own mom. It's either us," I pointed at my stomach, "or your mom." He growled in frustration and moved in front of me.

"That's bullshit, Mitchie! She's my mom! She raised me! You can't expect me to just drop her and never talk to her again. I'm not you!" The minute the words left his mouth, he brought his hand up to cover it.

"Mitchie, baby. I'm sorry. . ." I pushed his hand away and struggled to get out of the chair.

"Mac, please. . ." I shook my head, shoving him away before shutting the door behind me and walking back toward my room.

***

Chad and I didn't say a word to each other as we waited in the doctor's office. He kept glancing up at me, like he wanted too, then he would decide against it and look away.

"Ms. Halley! It's nice to see you again. Mr. Follet." The doctor bowed his head at Chad and kissed my hand.

"Dr. Lee, it's nice to see you again as well." I replied, smiling. He grinned as he slipped on his gloves.

"How have you been? Running into any problems lately?" I shook my head, laughing.

"Other then not being able to walk I've been great!" I responded. He nodded, chuckling to himself.

"Well, let's get started." The next hour went by pretty quick. He gave us a grin when he was done before excusing himself from the room.

"Are you going to talk to me? I've said I was sorry multiple times." Chad growled, standing up. I turned my head in the opposite direction and messed with the bracelet around my wrist.

"Mitchie, come on. You can't sit here and ignore me."

"What do you want me to say, Chad?" I finally asked, exhausted. He laid his hand on my stomach.

"I don't care. I just want you to talk to me again." He whispered, his lips brushing against mine. I pulled his face down so his lips would make contact with my own.

"I have the results!" Dr. Lee said loudly, walking back in. Chad took my hand and squeezed it as we looked at the doctor.

"So you see this." He handed us both an ultrasound. I suddenly remembered what my mom had told me when I was Yellerer, what she had said about being able to tell the sex of the child.

"It's a girl. Emilia." I said quietly, glancing over at Chad. He was staring down at the sonogram, rubbing his forehead.

"Yes, it's a girl. Here is the other." I took the second ultrasound and immediately gasped.

"A boy! Jackson!" I cried, smiling through the tears that streamed down my cheeks. Chad finally looked up, sighing in relief.

"One of each. Thank god." He smiled, setting the sonograms in my purse.

"You are free to leave, please don't hesitate to call me if you need anything." We both nodded. I smiled and turned to Chad, and for the first time all day I knew that we were both happy.

**

"Em and Jack." Chad said again. I smiled, nodding.

"So, I was out with David yesterday. One of the houses across the street from his is for sale." I stared at him, my eyebrows furrowing in confusion.

"I was thinking maybe a couple months after they're born we can try looking for a house." He said nervously. He took a sip from his wine, avoiding eye contact.

"We can't afford that, Chad. I still have to figure out a way to finish my education. And the babies, they are going to need tons of. . ."

"I make a lot of money now, Mac. It'll be okay. We'll have plenty." I sighed, laying my hands against my warm cheeks.

"I'll think about it. I'm gonna go get some sleep. Danny should be home soon, so you guys can just order something to eat." I pushed my chair back and got up, groaning. Chad helped me to our room, and on to the bed.

"I'll be in bed later." He kissed me gently before doing the same to my stomach and disappearing. I yawned and buried myself in the blankets. I knew that this would be the last week I would have any rest. The next month and half would be full of pain, screaming, crying, and then the babies would come.

"At least I'm not alone." I mumbled, fixing the blanket around me. I cleared my mind as quickly as I could and slowly fell into a peaceful sleep.

Chapter 20

The Last Song

I woke up to Chad climbing out of bed and rushing to the bathroom at two in the morning. Apparently there had been some stomach bug going around at his job and he had caught it.

"Are you okay?" I asked him when he fell back on to the couch. He turned to face me, making sure to keep his distance.

"Just peachy. Just fucking peachy."

****

"He's sick and doesn't want me to get catch whatever he has, so he said to come and visit you." I explained to my mom. Chad had been sick the last couple days and said I should go with Danny to visit our mom, to tell her the news about the babies.

"I can't believe you're having twins. Do you have names?" She asked, avoiding the subject of Chad entirely.

"Yeah. Jackson Chad Follet and Emilia Rose Follet." I answered, touching my stomach.

"Jackson? Like your father?" She growled. I nodded, my short lived happiness fading.

"He is my dad, Mom. And their grandfather."

"I understand, I guess." She grumbled, but I could tell she was a little hurt and offended. And despite it being wrong, I was actually a little glad to see her in as much pain as I had been.

"You are keeping them, right?"

"Yeah, Mom. We already have the nursery painted and everything. Chad's been working his ass of to help with the rent and buying stuff for the babies and me. Maybe that's why he got sick, because he's been working himself to death and his immune system was down." I said the last part more to myself then to her. As if on cue, my phone rang. I picked it up, hoping it was Chad with good news.

"Hello?"

"McKayla." I could feel my whole body stiffen at the voice.

"Rose." I snapped, earning strange looks out of my mom and brother.

"I've been informed that my son was sick. I thought I would check on him." She said quietly.

"I don't know how you got my number, but Chad does have his own phone." I hung up before I could hear whatever she was going to reply with. I gave my brother a quick nod and he smiled at my mom.

"We better get going, Mom. We'll see you soon." He kissed her cheeks then hugged her before he helped me out of the hospital, shaking his head to himself.

***

I yawned as I put my coat up and turned to the living room. Chad was sitting on the couch, eating chips as he watched a movie.

"You look better." I stated. I kissed him as I walked by and he smiled like a child.

"I feel better now. How was the visit?" I shrugged.

"It was okay. . . until your mom called." He frowned, grabbing his phone off the table.

"She called me earlier too, said she was going to call and apologize."

"Well she didn't. She only ruined my day." I snapped. I didn't actually give her a chance to say anything though. . .

"Calm down, babe. I'll let her know that you aren't feeling that great and that's why you snapped at her." I sat on the couch beside him, my lips turning down into another frown.

"How do you know I snapped. . ."

"Danny's got a big mouth." I nodded, smiling a little.

"Yeah, he doesn't know how to shut up." His eyes were lit with humor as he wrapped his arm around me.

"I was talking to a friend from work yesterday, he invited us to a barbeque. He said you looked like you were about to pop, so he understands if we can't make it. I was wondering if you wanted to go." I snuggled against him, letting what he said sink in.

"When is it?"

"Saturday."

"I mean, the babies aren't do for at least another month. I think it'll be good for me to get some fresh air and not stress for a couple hours." I responded. He grinned, kissing my forehead. He looked ready to say something but the doorbell cut him off. He muttered something under his breath before walking toward the door.

He opened the door to reveal Louis, or at least part of him. His arms were filled with tons of multicolored gift bags and a giant teddy bear over his shoulder.

"This half is from my mom, this is from me, and the rest is from Rea." He grumbled, tossing it all on to the loveseat. I grunted as I got up and walked over to see what it was. Most of it was baby clothes or toys, but some of it was things for Chad and me.

"You look pregnant." Louis stated the obvious. I stuck my tounge out at him and held a cute onesy out to Chad.

"This is so cute!" Chad laughed at my expression and glanced over Louis's shoulder.

"You didn't happen to bring any food, did you? Danny won't go shopping until Sunday." Louis grinned and jogged out of the house for a moment. I dug through the rest of the presents while I waited, showing Chad most of them.

"Daddy's Daredevil? That fits." Chad commented on a red onesie for a boy. I slapped his arm and dropped it into bag.

"Pizza!" Chad yelled immaturely. I stood up s well and grabbed a piece from the box Louis was holding.

"So is that all you came here for, man? To drop off presents for us?" Louis shifted nervously.

"Louis, what's wrong?" I asked, setting the crust of my pizza on the table in the living room. He shook his bowed head, his hand clenched into a fist.

"I don't think it's a good idea to say. . ."

"Louis, just say it. What's going on?" Chad demanded, his eyes dark. Louis took a deep breath, glancing from my stomach then into my eyes.

"I can't, Chad. It'll give her another attack or worse. . ."

"Dammit, Louis! Just fucking say it!" Chad yelled, grabbing his friends shoulders roughly. Louis let out a shaky breath, and to my surprise turned his attention to Chad.

"I didn't know what it was. I thought it was just the cops checking out Mitchie's place again, but then I saw your mom's car and. . ." Chad had to grip on to the arm of the couch to brace himself for what was coming.

"I don't know, maybe she had a panic attack like Mitchie. Or maybe it was a heart attack. Chad," He grabbed his best friends arm. "Your mom was rushed to the hospital a couple hours ago and nobody knows if she's going to make it."

Chapter 21

Real World

"You don't understand, Chad. It's my fault." I cried again, slamming my hands against his chest. He gripped my wrists, shaking his head.

"It's not. Stop blaming yourself. You acted on what you felt, Mitchie. Leave it at that. My mom had a heart attack because she felt bad about what she said to you, not because you said anything to her. Now stop worrying, you'll hurt yourself and the babies." He wrapped his arms around me, his eyes scanning the waiting room. I must have dozed off because I was stirred awake by Chad standing up.

"How is she?" He asked, rushing over to the doctor. I sat in the chair, wiping the sleepiness from my eyes.

"Chad? Is she okay?" I questioned once he walked back over to me. He pulled me into a hug, not saying a word. I could feel worry building in my chest.

"Nic, is she. .. " He put his index finger against my lips.

"She's okay. The doctor said she needs rest. Let's go back to my house for tonight." I didn't reply, I was still in too much relief and shock. He grabbed his jacket from his seat before taking my hand and leading me out of the hospital.

*****

"I don't care! It hurts!" I screamed. Chad stared at me in sympathy, his hand squeezing mine. I knew that his hand was probably bleeding because of how much my nails were digging into his skin.

"Should I take you to the hospital? Mitchie, I can help. . ."

"Dr. Lee said it's normal. He. . . ah. . . said it's just them kicking. They want out as much as we want them out." I groaned, turning to face him. Chad sighed before laying down next to me, his hand resting on my stomach. And almost as if he was a magical god, the babies stopped kicking.

"They stopped." I gasped, shutting my eyes. He smiled, kissing me.

"Good, because I hate seeing you in pain." I stared at him, my hand in his hair.

"That was so cliché. I wish you could have these babies." He laughed.

"I don't. Oh god no." He shook his head, staring at me in horror.

"You're an idiot." I mumbled. He grinned, still shaking his head.

"I know. I know."

****

I stared back and forth between Louis and Chad. Next to each other they didn't look so different, they could have even been brothers. But as soon as Chad moved away, the sameness in their expressions as well as their figures changed.

"I'll be back in a couple hours. I promise." Chad said, kissing me quickly and patting his best friend on the shoulder. He was out the door before I could say goodbye.

"So. . . what do pregnant women do?" Louis asked, shifting uncomfortably.

"The same thing everyone does, idiot. We can watch a movie." I suggested, turning on Chad's Wii so I could see what was on Netflix.

"Okay." Louis muttered, sitting on the couch beside me. We decided on watching the first Avengers movie. Louis passed out about half way through the movie, so I turned it off and went into the kitchen. I turned my computer on and looked up online school's. I knew I wouldn't be able to go back to a normal high school, not with two kids.

"I'm starving." I moaned to myself, dragging myself into the kitchen. I raided the fridge and crossed my arms when I couldn't find anything to eat. Chad had taken any type of junk out of the house so I couldn't eat it. I rolled my eyes and grabbed a water bottle out of the fridge. My poor kids were going to have a super over protective father.

"I am ho. . . he seriously fell asleep?" Chad asked, shutting the door behind him. I didn't look up when I replied.

"Yeah, like ten minutes ago. He sleeps like a log. Not a very good caretaker. He's definitely not baby sitting for us." I told him. He walked over and dropped a take out box in front of me.

"Oh, Chad. You are such a life saver!" I cried, digging into my food immediately. He chuckled as he sat down beside me, slowly opening his own food.

"What are you doing?"

"Looking at online schools. I need to finish my education, Chad. I am not going to be a horrible role model for my kids. College is different, I'll probably wait a while. But I only have on year of high school left. I have to complete it." He nodded, not looking at me.

"I wish I could too. But I don't have any free time, and honestly I don't really care. But I'm glad you want to do it." I smiled sadly at him, trying to ignore the sad look in his eyes.

"How's your mom?" I asked, changing the subject.

"Okay, I guess. She feels horrible about what she did to you." I could tell he was hiding something.

"What is it, Chad? Is something wrong?" I reached across the table to grab his hand, staring at him in worry.

"Everything is fine. It's just . . . well you know my mom is living alone and isn't working, she won't be able to pay the rent or anything. And she'll be lonely." He stopped, looking into my eyes to see if I understood what he was saying.

"I'll be worrying about her constantly. Mitchie, my mom wants to know if she can stay with us, just until she gets back on her feet. She said she'd help with the babies, and with anything either of us needed." I opened my mouth in shock.

"Chad, I don't know. We can barely feed ourselves. How can we support both kids and your mom along with us with only your income?" He sighed, running a hand through his hair.

"It'll only be for a couple months. I promise. You won't even know she's there. I'll figure everything out, Mitchie. Don't worry." I shut my eyes, my appetite suddenly gone. I pushed my food away and stood up, kissing Chad on my way past him.

"Get Louis a blanket. I'm going to bed early tonight." He gave me a nod before standing up and grabbing his best friend a blanket out of the closet.

"Mitchie?" I turned to face him.

"Yeah?"

"Everything will be fine." The only thing I could do was pray that he was right.

Chapter 22

Night Drive

"Get out! Go!" I snapped, throwing my pillow at Chad. He leaned back against the door frame, his lips set in a thin line.

"Mitchie, you have to tell me if you think you're about to pop. The expected date is only a week and a half. You could have them at any time." I threw another pillow, but he dodged that one as well.

"Just go to your stupid, irritating mother!" I replied, burying my face in my pillow.

"I know you've been having issues with her but. . ."

"Issues? She think she fucking owns the place, Chad! She's constantly telling me what I have to do, how I should sit down so the babies will be okay. She is driving me insane!" I screamed, sitting upright. He walked over and sat on the edge of the bed, resting his hand on my leg.

"She's only looking out for you, Mac. She. . ."

"No! She can't wait until these two are out." I pointed at my stomach, "She'd love to take them away and try to raise them! She thinks I'm going to be a horrible mother! She doesn't. . ." Chad slammed his hand over my mouth, glaring at me.

"Stop it! I understand that you hate her, Mitchie. But you need to calm down. Do you want to hurt the babies?" I shook my head, relaxing a little. He sighed and laid his forehead against mine.

"I'll talk to her, okay?" I wrapped my arms around his neck, my head on his shoulder.

"I'm sorry for snapping at you. It's just your mom and the hormones and just everything!" I whispered. He pulled away and pushed me gently back on the bed.

"I'll be right back, I'm just going to talk to her." I nodded and he disappeared from the room, leaving me to stare up at the plain white ceiling by myself.

*****

I woke up screaming in pain, and completely aware that the bed was soaked around me. Chad, who had passed out at the foot of the bed, jumped to his feet, startled.

"Mitchie? Hey, are you okay?" I shook my head, pushing the blanket off so he could see the wet sheets.

"Shit. You're water broke?" He guessed, rushing across the room to grab my bag.

"Ah!" I cried again, holding my stomach. Chad ran back over to me, helping me out of the bed.

"Mom!" Chad yelled, then shouted what was happening after it. I let out another cry as he helped me to the car outside.

"It hurts!" I whimpered, gripping Chad's hand. He shut the door on my side and walked around the car, starting it without putting his seat belt on.

"I know, Mac. Just take deep breaths, in and out." He kept glancing sideways at me the whole way to the hospital. I was still screaming when he jumped out of the car and ran into the hospital. He ran back out, a few nurses with a stretcher behind him.

"Chad! N. . . no!" I gasped as they pulled me out of the car. Chad squeezed my hand.

"It'll be okay. I'm right here."

****

"Good morning, Sunshine." Chad's deep voice stirred me out of my daze. I looked up, my eyes meeting his blue ones.

"Is. . . are they. . ."

"They're fine. Both healthy. Emilia was born at eleven fourty-eight and Jackson at twelve exactly." I smiled, groaning as I sat up. I looked around the room, searching for my babies.

"Come on. I'll take you to them." He helped me out of the bed, staring down at my now small figure. He laughed to himself as we walked down the dim lit hospital hallway. He stopped in front of a room filled with babies and a couple nurses.

"Mr. and Mrs. Follet I have. . ."

"W. .. we aren't married." I said quickly, earning a strange look out of Chad.

"Well, you both are free to go in and see them." We thanked her and walked into the room. I searched for Chad's last name and smiled when I found them next to each other. Chad reached down, and as gently as he could, picked up Emilia. I stared, my mouth opening.

"You can hold Jackson." I looked down at our crying son, his blue eyes mirroring Chad's.

I picked up up, my hands slightly shaking. The minute he was in my arms he stopped crying. I could feel my eyes burning as his small hand wrapped around my finger.

"Chad. . ." I whispered, looking back at him. He was staring at our daughter with and expression that probably matched mine.

"I. . . they're beautiful." He said. I agreed and moved to stand by him, running my hand along my daughter's cheek.

"I. . . I don't even know what to say." I stated. He set Emilia back down and I did the same with Jackson. He touched my cheek just as gently as he had touched our daughters.

"I love you. I wish I could take back everything hurtful thing I did and said. I wish that we both could just forget that it ever happened, but we can't. I just want to know if you can try and forgive me." I touched his lips with my index finger.

"Of course. I love you too, Chad." I replied, before letting him pull me into a bone crushing hug, ending in us both laughing when Jackson and Emilia started crying at the same time. We exchanged a look before smiling and picking our kids up, and I knew in that moment, that neither of us would ever let go.

Chapter 23

Happy Endings

I looked around the nursery, smiling. It really did look beautiful. The two cribs were pushed back against the wall, pink blankets in one and blue in the other. The rocking chair, which at the moment had a stuffed bear on it, was beside Jack's crib.

"I did a good job." Chad said from behind me, arrogantly.

"You did." I replied, yawning as I walked over to the crib. We had only been home about a week, but I, as well as the twins had already adjusted. Chad had even put a bed in the room for us, just in case we had to come and sleep in here.

"I. . . um, wanted to talk to you. It's something I probably should have told you back at the hospital." I flipped around, staring at Chad angrily. I knew he had been keeping something from me.

"What? Chad, what's going on?" He scratched the back of his neck, sitting on our bed.

"W. . . when Jack came out they found your umbilical cord wrapped around his neck. I. . . they got it off, but they said it could effect him. They also said it's too early to tell if it did any damage." I stared at him in horror, my hand flying over my mouth.

"And you thought that waiting to tell me this was okay? Chad he's our son! I want to know everything. . ."

"I didn't think it really mattered. B. . . but yesterday when I went to feed Em, he was silent. He was awake, but he didn't cry or anything. I. .. I was scared so I asked my mom and she said to talk to you." I let out a cold laugh.

"Oh, so you can go and tell your mom about Jack, but you can't tell me about my own son? That's fucking it, Chad. Either she leaves or I leave with the kids. I can't deal with her hovering over me, or you talking to her about things you should be talking to me about." He flew off the bed, his hands clenching into fists.

"You can't threaten me, McKayla! I help pay for this fucking house! Where are you going to go? Huh? How dare you threaten to take them away! She's my mother, Mac! I'm not going to choose." I pushed him away from me and walked over to the cribs and grabbed a duffel bag from the ground.

"What are you doing?" Chad growled from behind me.

"I'm leaving. I'll go stay with David! I don't need you, Chad! I am not some charity case that you need to pay for." I snapped back. I heard him let out a frustrated growl as I tossed Jack's clothes into my bag.

"Mitchie, don't leave." His voice was quieter now. I froze where I was sitting beside the cribs.

"Mitchie, please. I'm sorry." He whispered, approaching me.

"I'll give her some money so she can find herself a cheap apartment. She'll be gone tomorrow." He added. I dropped the bag back on the ground and threw myself into his arms.

"You promise you'll tell me everything from now on?"

"I promise." He whispered back.

****

"Hey, Daddy." I said, standing awkwardly beside his hospital bed. I bit my lip as I sat down in the chair beside it.

"You would be surprised at how much has changed in the last year. I've attempted to talk to mom again. Of course there's also the twins and Chad." I went on, laughing nervously.

"Dan and Dave keep telling me I should just let them take you off, let you rest in peace. Even Chad has started to say so." I wiped a stray tear from my eye, shaking my head.

"I could never bring myself to say yes. I thought you'd wake up, that you would be able to see my kids, be able to see Chad and I together.

That you'd get to walk me down the isle." I could feel a lump forming in my throat.

"But it's been almost a year, Daddy. And you haven't showed any signs of waking up. You tried to end your life, so maybe you wanted to die. So I'm not going to be the one to stop you from going wherever it is you go when you die." I let go of his hand, standing back up.

"Goodbye, Dad. I hope you can watch us from wherever you are going. I love you." I bowed my head as I left the room and the nurse went in. Even as I hurried down the hall and tried to get out as fast as I could, I couldn't escape the sound of my dad's monitor flat lining.

****

"Are you okay, Mac?" I rolled over so Chad couldn't see me crying.

"Mitchie?" He asked again. Finally he gave up on talking to me and flipped me over so I was facing him.

"Why are you crying?" He wiped the tears from my cheeks, his eyes wide with worry and wonder.

"I told them to unplug my dad today." I whimpered. To my surprise, he didn't look at me in sympathetically, but in anger. His jaw was clenched so hard I was scared he was going to hurt himself.

"So it's that ass that's got you crying? Mitchie, he's in a better place. He wanted to die, so let him rest in peace. Remember him for the good times you had together." I buried my face against his bare chest, sobbing.

"Mitchie. . ." He sighed, but he didn't say anything else. He just let me cry on him, covering him in tears.

"I'm sorry." I finally said when I was done crying.

"Don't apologize, baby. I understand. I. . . it just kind of ruined what I had planned for this weekend." I lifted my head off his chest, cocking my head.

"What did you have planned?" He stroked my hair, his lips tugging up into a smile.

"I was going to take you and the kids to the park and I was going to get all corny and get down on one knee. I had this whole speech prepared." I could feel my heart start racing at his words.

"You were going to propose?" I asked.

"I mean, we are already a family. I just wanted you to have my last name too. McKayla Follet." I liked the way the name sounded. I crawled on top of him, smiling despite how sad I still felt.

"I like the way that sounds." I whispered, leaning down to kiss him. His hands slid so that he was gripping my hips.

"Mmm, yeah it sounds good, doesn't it?" He pushed me back down on to the bed beside him, smiling.

"Mrs. Follet, would you like to go set up the baby monitor or should I?" He asked, in a mock English accent. I slapped his arm and hopped out of the bed.

"How about we both go?" I suggested. He followed me out of the room, nodding.

"Sounds great to me."

Chapter 24

Epilogue

"I'm gonna get you!" Chad teased, scooping our daughter up from her crib. She started giggling as she kicked at him.

"I'm gonna. . ."

"Chad, I'm going to hit you if you don't stop playing around and go get ready." He turned to me, pouting as he gestured toward our daughter.

"Emmy, Mommy's being mean." He said, hugging her. I shook my head at how childish he was acting as I took Emilia and set her in her carrier.

"You are acting like a three year old." I told Chad, fixing his tie.

"I'm just trying to lighten the mood. This is the happiest occasion you know." He replied, glaring down at me.

"I know, Chad. But we have to go. You have to stand as one of the witnesses. It'll be okay. Emmy will be here for you to play peek-a-boo with when we get home." I winked at him, leaning down to pick up both of the carriers. Chad wrapped his arms around me from behind.

"I've also got you when I get home. We're going out tonight, remember? Louis's watching the twins." I sighed, mentally scolding myself for not remembering.

"Yeah. You know I've had a lot on my mind since my dad's funeral." I turned to look at him as he nodded.

"I know, Mac. You just look so damn sexy with that ring on your finger I want to make it official." I laughed, shaking my head as we walked out of the nursery.

****

"If I find you asleep I will beat you with that giant teddy bear, then beat you with this carrier." Louis threw his hand over his chest, staring at me like I was a killer.

"Yes, Ma'am! I promise I will stay awake all night, Ma'am!" He saluted me. I slapped his hand and handed him the carrier.

"Sometimes Jack has a hard time sleeping, you have to hold him until he falls asleep." I said, handing him the carriers. He nodded.

"You two have fun and don't worry, I have this all under control." I gave Chad a look telling him I didn't quite believe his best friend before he patted my back and pushed me toward the door.

"I better get her out of here before she changes her mind. I've been trying to do this for like three months." Chad said to Louis, grinning. Louis said something back but I was outside before I could hear what it was. Once we were in the car, Chad leaned over and kissed my cheek.

"Mrs. McKayla Follet, for the longest time I thought that I was a freak. That I was just some kid that got molested by his aunt. Then you came along, you showed me how to love. What love was. I wasn't ready to be a dad, not even close. But with you by my side, I knew that I could do it." I waited for him to continue, but he didn't. Instead he started the car, a devious smirk on his face.

"Chad, what was that speech about? Chad, where are we really going?" He grinned, taking my hand in his.

"Vegas." My eyes grew wide as my head whipped toward him.

"Chad, we are not eloping! No way! David and Destiny will kill me! And our moms will lose it." He shrugged, as if he didn't care.

"It's our choice. You will be Mrs. Follet before your birthday in a couple days. I guess you could say I'm kidnapping you." He said, laughing. I raised an eyebrow, slowly starting to calm down.

"You aren't kidnapping me if I want to be with you." I said, grinning. He turned the radio on before grabbing my hand again. I turned to look out the window, as all the city lights turned into blurs around us. I thought about Em and Jack back at Louis's house, wondering if he knew we wouldn't be back for a few days. I thought about my mom and how I was slowly starting to forgive her for what she did, and about Chad's mom who I wasn't to sure of yet. I even thought about my dad and how I smiled to myself as they lowered him into the ground, thinking about how great of a father he had been.

Finally I thought about me and Chad. We were by no means the "It" couple. We were freaks, crazies. Sometimes I still question on how we ended up together. Was it fate? Was it coincidence? Whenever I thought about how far we'd come in the last year, I always came up with the same answer. We knew each other's dirty little secrets, and we loved each other for each and every one of them.

Chapter 25

The Devil with A Soul~ Chad

(13 Years Old)

"Chad!" My mom's ear piercing screech pulled me out of my daze and I moved away from the window.

"What is it, Mom?" I asked, walking into the kitchen.

"Mrs. Yeller called and said that Mitchie had another outburst. I was wondering if you could go check on her."

"Why, Mom? She isn't my problem." I snapped back a little too quickly. I tried to push the weird feeling I got in my stomach at the mention of the name.

"Please, honey. You know how her dad is." I rolled my eyes and gave in to my mom's orders.

"Fine, god." I mumbled as I grabbed my leather jacket and slipped outside without another word. As if on cue, I saw Mitchie walking home from school on the other side of the street, her arms wrapped around herself as the cold breeze blew her hair around her wildly.

"Mitchie! Hey!" I called out. Her head whipped toward me as she stopped dead in her tracks. I approached her slowly, ignoring the weird feeling in my chest again.

"W. . . what do you want, Chad? Are you just going to laugh at me again?" She asked, her dark eyes glistening. I could feel guilt biting at me.

"No, I wanted to see if you were okay. I know Kim was being a bitch and. . ."

"And no one tried to stop her. I don't even care anymore, Chad. Because you push me around just as much as she does." I shook my head as she started to walk away.

"Mitchie, wait!" I grabbed her arm, and she elbowed me hard.

"Stay away from me, Chad!" I gripped my stomach, hunched over, as I watched her walk fast back toward her house. I sighed and walked down the sidewalk, cussing to myself as I kicked a rock in front of me.

"It's your fault, man! You take all of your anger out on her." Louis had told me almost a year ago. He wasn't wrong. He was the only one that knew what my aun. . . Michelle did to me. He was the only was who gave a shit. . . other than Mitchie. I knew that she would care, that she would feel bad for me, even though her life was far more fucked up then mine.

I stopped dead in my tracks when I heard yelling from Mitchie's house. I was about to run up the stairs when she came back outside, blood sliding down the left part of her face.

"Mitchie!" I gasped, reaching for her arm. She pushed me away, shaking her head.

"I told you to leave me alone! Just go!" She screamed, her beautiful hazel eyes pooling with tears.

"Mitchie, you have to let me help." I whispered, slipping out of my jacket and ripping the sleeve of my t shirt, before putting it to the side of her head.

"Why are you being nice to me? Because Louis and all of your stupid friends aren't here?" She snapped. I frowned, looking away. She wasn't wrong. That was part of the reason I treated her the way I did, because I didn't want to look like some little bitch in front of Louis.

"You can go now, Chad. The blood clotted. I have to go find someone to buy liquor for me." She said quietly, pushing my hand away.

"Your dad did this?" She gave me a weird look.

"Of course he did. Go a head and go tell all your little friends about little miss bitchie Mitchie." She added sarcastically before stalking off. I watched after her, my hand clenching around the piece of bloody cloth in my hand. I let out a growl before tossing it to the ground and stomping up the steps and throwing open Mitchie's door.

"McKayla, I told you too. . ." Mr. Halley shut his mouth when he saw me standing in the doorway. I must have looked intimidating to him. I was pretty tall for a fourteen year old, and I had started to go to the gym and lift weights with Louis recently.

"Listen, you fucking asshole. If I ever see you lay a hand on Mitchie again, I will make you wish you never fucking had a daughter." I walked over and punched him as hard as I could, his hand immaturely went to his gushing nose.

"Stay the fuck away from her!" I snarled, then took off out of the house, slamming the door behind me. I punched the car, glaring at my reflection in it. I could slowly feel my self starting to calm down as I pictured Mitchie's face. How she would look at me like I was a monster for hitting her dad. I started walking back toward my house, shaking my head.

Why did I care about what she thought? She was just some stupid little abused girl.

"Because you love that stupid little girl." I growled to myself under my breath. And I knew that I couldn't deny it anymore. Somehow the little black haired devil had managed to worm her way into my heart and take it from me.

"But you can't let her get hurt because of you." I told myself. I took a deep breath and decided in that moment that I wouldn't let myself get close to her, I couldn't. Because I loved her, and all that mattered to me at that moment was that she was okay. And if she had anything to do with me I know she wouldn't be.

Chapter 26

Just Because You Can

"Chad, get her!" I cried, ready to pull out my hair. Our three year old daughter ran passed him, but he was too quick for her. He picked her up and kissed her forehead.

"I swear to god that you love her more then Jack." I said, more to myself then him. His eyes darkened at the accusation.

"He's my son, Mitchie. You know I would never. . ."

"I don't want to talk about this again. Jack's at the hospital for the third time this year, aren't you even the least bit worried?" I snapped at my husband. He shifted Emilia on his waist and shook his head.

"Mitchie, you can't keep worrying. You'll kill yourself. He'll be okay. You heard the doctor, he said Jack is just Autistic. He isn't going to die." He replied, reaching for my hand. I pushed him away, throwing my hands in the air.

"When you decide to actually give a shi. . . crap about your son come to the hospital." I stormed out of the house without waiting for him to reply.

****

"Hi, Jack Jack!" I said, kneeling down to kiss my son's head. He held up a block with an M on it, giggling.

"Yeah, M is for Mommy!" I exclaimed, hugging him. He giggled again and put the block down before picking one up with a D on it. I ruffled his mop of black curls.

"Daddy's not here, baby boy. He's with Emmy." Jack frowned, almost as if he understood. He slowly picked up a block with a B on it. I frowned, shaking my head.

"What does that mean?" He opened his mouth to say something but he dropped the block and pouted when nothing came out.

"Hey, it's all right, baby boy. . ." He started pointing at himself, smiling.

"What? Is something wrong Jack? Baby. . ." He nodded again, picking up the block and holding out in front of my stomach.

"No, Jack Jack. That's my tummy. That's a T not a B." He started to pout again and sat back down in his small chair.

"How is he doing?" A voice asked from behind me. I smiled at the pediatrician.

"He seems to be doing pretty well with the blocks. He keeps holding up the B block, though. Maybe he's trying to say he's a boy?" I asked him. The doctor nodded and knelt down in front of Jack.

"Hey, Buddy. You can try and talk to Mommy, you know. She wants you to talk to her." Jack lifted his head slowly, his blue eyes burning into mine.

"Baby. Mommy has baby." He whispered. I looked up at the doctor, frowning.

"What is he trying to say?"

"I think he's trying to tell you he thinks your pregnant." I blinked in shock, my hands going to my stomach.

"He couldn't possibly know that, could he?" I asked. The doctor rubbed his beard, shaking his head.

"He is quite intelligent, Mrs. Follet. He could have observed the way you were acting, or maybe he saw something on TV." He replied.

"Can I take him home? Is good enough to. . ."

"Yes. Although I was hoping that Chad would be here with you so we could talk. All the same, I guess I could just speak to you." I waited for him to go on as I picked up Jack's toys and tossed them into my bag.

"I have come to realize that Emilia has been playing around with Jack, maybe a little too much. I think that's what caused his outburst. I think you should try to talk to her, try to explain that he's special." I glared at the doctor as I stood up.

"So you're telling me I have to keep my daughter away from my son? That isn't fair, they are. . ."

"Mrs. Follet, please let me finish. I believe that Jack may be ready for you to start teaching. His mind will develop quicker then his sister's. And although it may seem early to you, like he isn't learning anything, he is." I sighed, pushing my bangs out of my eyes as I headed back toward the door.

"Thank you, Dr. Lee." He nodded. I fought the urge to go off on him as I hurried out of the hospital.

***

"Mitchie, calm down. He's only trying to look out for Jack." Chad whispered, rubbing my back. I turned to face him, shaking my head.

"He's a freak, Chad. My baby is going to be bullied and told he's a freak because he's smarter and a little stranger looking that everyone else. I don't want my baby to be bullied." Chad ran his fingers through my hair, closing his eyes.

"I know, Mitchie. We're going to have to wait until we can be sure that he won't just grow out of it." I sighed, sitting on our bed.

"Jack thinks I'm pregnant." I said as quietly as I could.

"What? Did you just say our three year old son thinks your pregnant?" Chad started laughing then stopped when he saw my face.

"You're serious?" He asked. I nodded, staring down at the toy covered floor.

"I. . . I have been feeling strange all week, Chad. We thought it might have been a flu or something, but what if he's right. What if I am pregnant?" Chad shrugged, falling on to the couch beside me.

"At least we'll be prepared this time." I smiled, turning to look at him.

"Hopefully."

CPSIA information can be obtained
at www.ICGtesting.com
Printed in the USA
LVHW081250101122
732762LV00014B/866

9 781804 778579